THE CATTLEMAN'S UNSUITABLE WIFE

Pam Crooks

MILLS & BOON

First published in Great Britain 2011
Harlequin Mills & Boon Limited,
Eton House, 18-24 Paradise Road, Richmond, Surrey TW9 1SR

© Pam Crooks 2009

ISBN: 978 0 263 88235 3

Harlequin Mills & Boon policy is to use papers that are natural, renewable and recyclable products and made from wood grown in sustainable forests. The logging and manufacturing process conform to the legal environmental regulations of the country of origin.

Printed and bound in Spain
by Litografia Rosés, S.A., Barcelona

Pam Crooks grew up in the heartland of Nebraska's sandhills, where the code of the Old West still runs strong. She read her first romance novel way back in the '70s, and she's still reading them today. Even better, she loves to write them, too. Since 2001 she has had over ten historical Western romances hit the shelves. She is one of the founders of the popular website Petticoats & Pistols, a ten-author blog dedicated to promoting Western romance: www.petticoatsandpistols.com. Pam still resides in Nebraska, with her husband (who is not a cowboy) and their growing family—four daughters, two sons-in-law and three grandchildren.

Contact Pam via e-mail from her website, www.pamcrooks.com, or snail mail at PO Box 540122, Omaha, NE 68154, USA.

Prologue

Montana Territory, Spring 1883

Woodrow Baldwin glared up at the words burned into the wooden beam above him.

Wells Cattle Company.

God, the sight of that name sickened him.

The beam hung over the entrance to one of the largest ranches in the territory of Montana. And here he was, looking down the lane that led to the main house. From the outside in, just like always.

Thanks to that no-good, womanizing father of his.

Sutton Wells owned the WCC and paid Woodrow to keep his sorry ass out of sight. Paid right handsome, too. Month after month, year after year. For most of Woodrow's pathetic life.

Well, that was going to change. Woodrow had gotten real tired of being kicked aside, like shit off his father's boots. He had as much right to the Wells's empire as Trey did.

Woodrow's lip curled at the thought of his older half brother. The son Sutton loved best.

His belly tightened with hate for both of them. He delved into a shirt pocket, found a match and lit himself a quirley to get through it. While blowing out the flame, he caught sight of a rider heading toward him.

He tensed. Strange time for callers. The sun had almost set for the day. The rider wouldn't be out this way if he didn't intend to turn into the lane leading toward the Wells's home.

Sure enough, seeing Woodrow, the man reined in. Woodrow took his time exhaling and decided the rider wasn't one of his father's cowboys. He dressed different, wore a flat-brimmed hat, rode a mangy-looking roan.

"Howdy," Woodrow said, relaxing.

The stranger inclined his head. "This where Sutton Wells lives?"

A faint accent laced the low-spoken query, and Woodrow wondered where the rider was from.

"Yep," he said.

"Is he home?"

Woodrow's glance swung to the square window in the distance, on the far left side of the house. A light shone through the glass, which glowed brighter the darker the night got.

Sutton's office. The only room Woodrow had ever been in. The old man had refused to let him step foot anywhere else inside that big house of his.

"He's there," Woodrow said, nursing another round of resentment.

"You have business with him?" the stranger asked.

"Yep."

"So do I."

Woodrow regarded the man, noted how his skin seemed a tad darker than most folks 'round these parts.

"What kind of business?" he demanded.

For a long moment, the stranger didn't respond. Then, he straightened, squared his shoulders and jerked his chin up.

"I'm his son," he said.

Stunned, Woodrow stared.

"But I don't think he knows I am," the rider added.

"What the hell are you talking about, mister? How come he don't know you're his son?"

"That's one of the things I intend to ask him. I only found out myself a short time ago."

In the dusk, Woodrow could see the flare of the man's nostrils, the fury—or was it pain?—that shimmered from him, like heat off simmering tar.

Another son for Sutton Wells.

Well, well, well. Now wasn't that just too rich?

Seemed the old man had a hard time keeping his pants up around the ladies. Which got Woodrow to wondering just how many other little Wells bastards were out there, populating God's green earth.

Suddenly the ludicrousness of it all hit him. He threw back his head and guffawed.

"Why are you laughing?" the stranger demanded, his fist clenched on the reins.

Took Woodrow a spell before he could catch his breath. Once he managed it, he leaned from the saddle and extended his hand.

"Name's Woodrow Baldwin," he said through his grin. "The old man is my father, too."

The dark shape didn't move.

"That's not funny," the stranger snapped.

"It's the truth." Woodrow kept his arm outstretched. "Reckon I'm entitled to know your name, seeing's we're brothers and all."

"Brothers."

"That's right. You and me."

The stranger appeared to struggle with incredulity. Finally he muttered an oath and reached out; their hands met and clasped.

"Mikolas Vasco," he said.

"Mikolas." Woodrow tested the unusual word on his tongue and drew back. Since his quirley had burned down to his fingers, he took a last puff and tossed the stub aside. "Glad to meet you, Mikolas. Smoke?"

"Thanks."

Woodrow rooted inside his shirt pocket again and withdrew two cigarettes. Lighting one, he handed it over and lit the second for himself.

Both drew in long drags. Questions buzzed in Woodrow's head, curiosity about his newfound sibling's past, his intentions for the future, for the meeting ahead with the man whose parentage they shared.

But Woodrow figured there'd be plenty of time to ask questions later. For now, they just needed to get used to the idea that the same blood ran in their veins. At least, half of it.

They smoked in silence, and in the passing minutes, he sensed the tension growing in Mikolas. Curiosity got the best of Woodrow, after all. He squinted an eye through the veil of smoke.

"You plan on letting ol' Sutton know you're alive and kicking?" he asked.

"That's exactly what I'm going to do."

They both turned and studied the imposing shape of the house silhouetted on the horizon. And the light burning in that window on the far left.

"You're going to talk to him, too?" Mikolas asked.

Woodrow intended to talk all right. Whatever it took to get Sutton Wells to listen.

"Yep," he said.

"Then why are you sitting out here, on the road?" Mikolas asked.

"Just waiting until it's dark."

"Why?"

"Easier that way."

"How?"

Impatience flitted through Woodrow at the stream of questions.

"It just is, that's all," he snapped.

Over the years, he'd learned the hard way what it took to get Sutton Wells to listen to him. He'd learned, too, the depth of the shame, the contempt, the man felt at having Woodrow for a son.

"How old are you?" Woodrow demanded.

"Twenty-five."

"Twenty-five?" He drew back in surprise. "Well, hell. So am I."

Mikolas grunted with his own glowering surprise. "Selfish bastard cared nothing for our mothers except to use them for his pleasure."

Woodrow's mama had told him how Sutton's wife had died a couple of years after Trey was born. Sutton had never remarried, but after his wife's death, the tomcat had gone prowling, adding kittens to his litter. Instead of doing right by them, as a good father should, he'd sauntered away and left them to fend for themselves.

Woodrow figured he and Mikolas were the same

age, but Woodrow had more experience. And that put him in charge.

"Listen up, Mikolas. It's dark now, and that's the best way to ride up to the house. When no one can see us."

"I don't care if anyone sees us."

"You would if one of his damned outfit starts shooting at us. Or the old man throws us out himself."

Mikolas appeared taken aback. "He wouldn't do that. We're his sons. His family."

"Family don't have nothing to do with it. I'm telling you, he'll throw us out." Woodrow knew it firsthand, and he had the scars to prove it. "That's why we're going up there my way. Let me do the talking, y'hear?"

"I don't need you—"

"The hell you don't. The old man never took well to having me as his son, and he sure as hell won't take to having you for one, either."

"But Trey is different, isn't he?" Mikolas said, a sneer creeping into his voice.

"Now you're getting it." Hate gurgled again, a jealousy so thick and rampant Woodrow near choked from it. "Trey has always been different."

The favorite.

Everyone knew the Wells Cattle Company would be Trey's one day. Sutton Wells's firstborn son. Groomed to hold the reins to the family empire.

A family of two.

One father. One son.

Well, that was going to change. And time was a-wastin'.

"Let's go," Woodrow ordered, throwing the last of his cigarette into the weeds. His hand grasped the butt of the Colt slung to his hips. "And keep your mouth shut, y'hear? I'll let you know when you can talk."

This time, Mikolas didn't argue. Woodrow nudged his mount through the darkness, a slow, steady pace down the road toward that window with the glowing light.

Farther away on the ranch grounds, the indecipherable sound of laughter and voices drifted from a low-lying structure. The WCC bunkhouse. The cowboys would be turning in soon, in readiness for a dawn rising. They wouldn't be out to notice anything out of the ordinary, and Woodrow dismissed them.

He channeled his concentration on that office window instead. Gesturing to Mikolas, he pulled up beside bushes growing down the length of the house. The shadows were deeper here. Black as pitch. They dismounted and tied the leathers to branches.

Somewhere, a coyote howled, but a quick check revealed no one about. Woodrow kept his hand on his weapon, but he felt no fear. No apprehension. He knew what to do. What to expect.

Their boot soles scraped softly on the wooden porch. Woodrow withdrew his Colt from his holster with one hand, noiselessly turned the front doorknob with the other. He didn't bother knocking, and Mikolas's breathing quickened behind him. Clearly the man had never broken into someone's house before.

Woodrow smirked and stole inside. A gentle click indicated Mikolas pulled the door carefully closed. Woodrow turned to the left, toward the light spilling out of Sutton Wells's office and onto the thick, crimson floral rug.

The old man sat at his big, polished desk, his head bent over a rectangular-shaped ledger. He made notations with a pencil, his work absorbing him so deeply he had no idea two of his sons were standing there. Watching him.

Despising him.

Mounted on the wall, a set of longhorns took prominence, their wide breadth a symbol of Sutton's fortune. Nearby, a huge map depicted the boundaries of the Wells Cattle Company within the territory of Montana. On another wall, in neat rows, framed pictures hung from their wires. Photographs of prized bulls and fine-blooded horses. Some with a young boy, staring into the camera. And still more of him all grown-up.

Trey. It was *always* Trey.

Woodrow's jealousy burned, and his glance slid

back to Sutton. The man tended to wear his hair long, just past the collar of his shirt, the sides swept back. The strands glinted thick and golden in the lamplight.

As thick and golden as Woodrow's.

Mama always said he had hair just like his daddy. Funny how they each tended to wear it the same way, too. Past the collar of their shirt and swept back at the sides.

Woodrow gritted his teeth.

"Sorry to interrupt you, Pop," he said in a tone slathered with mockery.

Sutton's head jerked up. Slowly he set down his pencil, straightened in his chair.

"Don't call me that," he said.

"Tsk, tsk." The words shouldn't have stung, but they did. Damn him. "Is that any way to talk to your own flesh and blood?" he taunted.

Sutton's glance dropped to the Colt pointed at him. He stood carefully. Lifted his glance again. "What do you want, Woodrow?"

A plethora of things he wanted, needed, jumped onto his tongue. But he swallowed them all.

"There's someone here you ought to meet," he said.

Mikolas took the cue. Stepped forward. Sutton's glance swung toward him.

"Who are you?" he demanded.

"My name is Mikolas Vasco."

"That supposed to mean something to me?"

Mikolas flinched, and Woodrow couldn't help feeling sorry for him some. No one knew better than Woodrow Baldwin how much Sutton's rejection hurt, and now Mikolas was getting a taste of it, too.

"He's your son, damn you," Woodrow snarled before Mikolas could speak. "One more of your bastards."

"I don't believe you."

"Doesn't matter if you do, it's the truth!" Woodrow yelled.

"Enough, Woodrow!" Mikolas barked the command. He braced his feet, clenched his fists and faced the man who'd fathered him square. "My mother's name was—"

"I don't give a rat's ass who she was," Sutton spat. He leaned forward, planted his broad hands on the desktop and speared Woodrow with a look so scathing, iron would've curled. "Just like I don't care about yours."

Woodrow's grip tightened on the revolver. His sweet mama was the only person who'd ever loved him, really loved him, and God, he was a hair-trigger away from pumping Sutton Wells full of lead.

"Get out," Sutton said. His cold gaze jumped between them. "Both of you. Or I'll have you strung up from the rafters so fast your teeth will sing."

"You're a heartless—" Mikolas grated.

His gaze swung toward him. "Go to hell."

Mikolas hissed in a breath, pivoted and strode toward the open doorway. "When you go first."

"Mikolas, damn it, get back here," Woodrow ordered.

But Mikolas kept going. Out of the office, into the hall and through the front door, giving it a good slam when he did.

Woodrow gritted his teeth. Blackmail would've been a helluva lot easier if this yellow-spined brother of his hadn't left.

"What do you want from me?" Sutton snarled.

"Everything I can squeeze out of you, old man."

"You're not getting a dime more."

"Double. I want the money *doubled.*"

"Get out."

"Or I go to Trey. I'll tell him everything. I swear it."

Sutton trembled. From fury? From fear? His hand moved.

Or did it?

Woodrow couldn't tell for sure.

"Leave Trey out of this," Sutton said, his voice a deep, rasping rumble. "We agreed."

"Double the money, Pop."

"I'll kill you for this."

Suddenly the desk drawer jerked open, Sutton's hand whipped inside, and Woodrow did the only thing he could. The one thing he'd dreamed of, fantasized about, and *ached* to do most all his life.

He pulled the Colt's trigger.

Chapter One

Three days later

"She's gone, Trey."

Trey Wells didn't acknowledge the quiet voice behind him, but kept his stare pinned on the crowd beyond the office window. The scores of men, women and children, dressed in somber black, gathered on his front lawn.

They'd come to pay their respects to his murdered father. Except the paying respects part was over, and only socializing remained. Sutton Wells's funeral had drawn folks from all over the territory. Once the shock of his death had dissipated, after their frenzied ruminating had ended, well, hell, they stayed to eat, drink and have a blaring good time.

"Trey?"

It was different for them, he supposed. They hadn't lost the only family they had left. They hadn't been robbed of their best friend. Sutton Wells was Trey's business partner, too. Co-owner of the mighty Wells Cattle Company.

A thousand times Trey asked himself who would want him dead. And why?

Why?

A thousand times, Trey vowed to find answers— and revenge.

A hand clasped his shoulder in a gentle but firm command for his attention. Trey shut down his morose thoughts and turned.

As foreman for the WCC, only Nubby Thomas would understand the depth of Trey's grief. He'd cowboyed with Trey's father in Texas, back in the forties when they were both between hay and grass in their years.

"She's gone," Nubby repeated. He spoke with his usual patience, but concern showed in his sunbrowned face.

Trey frowned. "Who?"

"Allethaire. Ricky saw her leavin' the ranch a few minutes ago."

Trey recalled how she'd argued with him again, and sudden irritation nipped along his nerve endings. In her snit, she'd left without telling him goodbye. Damn it, she should've given him the courtesy—and today, of all days. God knew she would've expected the same from him if the situation was reversed—and so would her father.

"Not like Paris to just up and leave like that without—" Trey began.

"He didn't go with her."

Trey shot a glance back to the front lawn and found Paris Gibson at the refreshment table talking to Gregory Carlton, a cattleman whose spread bordered the WCC's.

"Reckon he doesn't know she's gone," Nubby added.

Trey's frown deepened. Paris knew as much about his daughter as a father could. Trey had never met a father more loving. Or more protective.

"What do you mean he doesn't know she's gone?" Trey demanded. "She rode out here with him after the services."

"She didn't take their rig. Took one of our horses instead. Gave Ricky a story about wanting to go for a pleasure ride and that you'd be meeting her after a spell. But the way she took off, well, Ricky figured it wasn't no pleasure ride, like she said." Nubby hesitated. "He asked me to let you know."

Trey's mind worked through the news. Allethaire was an expert horsewoman. She'd ridden the ranch numerous times and enjoyed it when she did. It wouldn't be unusual for her to get the urge to ride.

But on the day of his father's funeral?

And why would she lie about Trey meeting up with her?

"Any idea where she went?" he asked.

"Apparently she didn't say, but she was headed east."

The words circled in his head. Allethaire Gibson was one of the finest women he'd had the pleasure to meet. Gracious and refined, beautiful and educated. Yet despite her considerable and obvious attributes, Trey had thought long and hard before asking her to marry him. She was as fragile as spun glass some days. Compared to other women he knew, she was sorely ill-suited to ranch life, too. Had he ever seen her break out in a sweat? Get dirt under her nails? Heft a basket of wet laundry onto her hip?

Not once.

In the end, it'd been the hydro-electric plant her father wanted to build on Wells rangeland that convinced Trey the marriage was a necessary endeavor. An arrangement destined to ensure a much-needed source of power for Montana—and growth for ranchers and farmers. The plant would seduce the Great Northern Railway, too, whose tracks would be invaluable for shipping crops and livestock to eastern markets.

Trey hoped the love for Allethaire would come later.

As time went on, though, he wasn't sure it ever would.

Her pampered life as Paris Gibson's daughter taught her to think of herself first and leave the consequences for later. She was prone to tender feelings and quick tears. In the brief period Trey had known her, he'd been victim once or twice to her theatrics.

Seemed she'd made him a victim again.

He slid a tight breath through his teeth. If she didn't return soon, he'd have to go after her, before she got herself good and lost. Montana Territory was a far cry from Minneapolis, where she'd been born and raised. She was accustomed to orderly streets and familiar landmarks. Out in the Montana wilds, she'd lose her sense of direction in no time.

"She's wanting you to give up the ranch, isn't she?" Nubby asked.

The old cowboy had been witness to Allethaire's innuendos a time or two. Her thinly veiled tantrums that came more often of late.

"Yes," Trey said.

Thinking of how she'd brought it up again, during the funeral luncheon, he turned back toward the window. In the distance, snow clung to the crests of the Bear Tooth Mountains like giant dollops of thick cream. But at the foothills, miles of rich grass stretched and swayed as far as the eye could see.

All of it, Wells rangeland.

Part of him expected to see her riding in, looking apologetic for leaving without telling him and ready to smother him with kisses for the indiscretion.

The other part knew he wouldn't. She'd want him to come for her instead. Say all the right things to soften her up. Give her the promise she craved.

A promise he couldn't make.

Nubby stepped to the window, too, and for a moment they stood, shoulder to shoulder. Both of them staring through the glass panes.

Commiseration threaded Nubby's silence. Understanding. Trey soaked it in, like balm on wounded skin.

"She thinks you can run the place without me." He lifted the crystal glass he held, then remembered he'd already drank the whiskey. He didn't bother going for more. "She said with Dad gone, there's no real reason for me to stay in Montana."

A small, choking sound escaped Nubby. The disagreement he declined to voice.

"She wants me to partner with Paris. Take over his business interests when he retires." Trey didn't normally blather on, but now the words spilled from his throat, like marbles from a jar.

"Can't see you wearing a fancy Hereford suit to work every day, Trey."

"No."

It wasn't in him. He was a cattleman, not an industrialist. The thought of crowded streets, tall brick buildings crammed onto city blocks and a sky dirtied from smoke belched from factory chimneys chilled him. Living by a clock every day, playing society games, watching his hands grow soft from a lack of hard, sweat-making work—hell, Allethaire may as well drop him into a pine box and bury him.

"Then again, won't be easy for a woman like her to live out here," Nubby went on. "She's never been bred for it."

Something Trey and his father had discussed often. But Sutton had dismissed Trey's concerns, claiming a woman like Allethaire brought too much into the marriage to worry about something as trivial as her getting used to life on the WCC. What woman wouldn't, eventually?

Trey had disagreed with his logic then, just as he did now.

"She doesn't want to learn." Trey sighed heavily at her self-centered contrariness. "I told her I wanted to cancel the engagement to give ourselves more time to think it through before we have a wedding."

"Sorry to hear that, Trey."

Trey's mouth quirked. Nubby wanted to mean the words, but deep down, he didn't.

"Reckon she's acting like she is because she's just scared from the trouble we've been having," Nubby ventured. "She probably needs time to sort through it."

Trey's father's death meant trouble, all right. So did the WCC cattle which had turned up missing. And then there were the men who'd argued with Sutton....

Trey had heard them right here in the office three nights ago, after he'd gone to bed. He'd frowned over it at the time, but hadn't intruded.

If only he had.

Hours later, he found his father dead, and Trey's gut churned with the certainty the strangers were responsible. The police were doing what they could, but Trey wanted justice, even if he had to ride with the posse himself to get it.

"If she's scared, she shouldn't have ridden off the ranch alone," he said. "Doesn't make sense why she's been gone so long."

Nothing did anymore.

Whatever her reasons for leaving, a demanding urgency built inside Trey, driven by the sudden and somber possibility whoever murdered Sutton Wells might very well strike at Allethaire—a twisted means of kicking Trey when he was already down.

"I'm going after her." He turned and set his glass down on the desk.

"Want me to go with you?" Nubby asked.

His foreman was still dressed in his Sunday best suit. He'd slicked his close-cropped gray hair with oil, shaved his cheeks smooth of its usual bristle. Trey could count on one hand the number of times the cowboy gussied himself up.

Damned unfortunate Trey's father's funeral had to be one of those times.

Nubby had been like a brother to Sutton. A friendship they shared most of their adult years. Trey could trust him with anything, including standing in for him with that crowd of funeral guests out on the front lawn.

"No," he said finally. "Stay here and take care of things. I'll be back as soon as I can."

Nubby was all he had left now. There was no one else.

Except for Allethaire. Maybe not even then, but if he didn't find her soon, he could lose her, too.

"I don't care about the agreement you make with him, Papa," Zurina Vasco said firmly, her feet braced against the wagon's rough ride to keep from toppling out of the seat. "I care only about the sheep. And so should you."

"Of course, I care about the sheep, 'Rina. You think I forget? When they are all I have left?"

His words prickled against her heart. He didn't mean them. Not really. It was just that he grieved deeply over losing her mother to the pneumonia only last month. He'd lost her brother, Mikolas, too, the very same day, from the shocking confession Mama made shortly before she died. Sometimes Zurina feared he could think of nothing else but his suffering.

Did he think she hadn't suffered, too?

She waited a moment for the hurt to pass.

"No, Papa," she said quietly. "You still have me."

But he didn't seem to hear. His face, browned by his Basque heritage and tinted deeper by the sun, showed his worry. "If he finds us, he might not let us use the valley again. And then what would we do? Where would we go?"

"A risk, yes." Even so, she shrugged at its insignificance. "But only a small one and not worth fretting over."

Trey Wells owned a sinful amount of land. They could camp for days near the river, give the sheep the precious water they needed and neither he nor his despicable father would ever know.

Zurina kept her beliefs to herself. She refused to speak Sutton Wells's name, even though Papa had a grudging respect for his son.

"I gave him my word, 'Rina. Stay in Sun River Valley. Trey Wells knows he can trust Gabirel Vasco—" Papa thumped his chest with a work-roughened fist "—so he gives us the grass, the water, for our sheep. And because I give my word, there is no trouble."

"Except the grass is too dry, and there is not enough water anymore." She slipped her arm though his and squeezed, softening her argument. She had, after all, convinced him to leave, hadn't she? "When the rain comes, then we'll go back to the valley."

The promise had been what finally convinced Papa to load up their sheep wagon and move their flock closer to Sun River. He'd given in only because he knew she was right. They had no other choice.

"Bah. The rain. Maybe it never comes." His mouth turned into a dejected frown beneath his thick, dark moustache.

She patted his hand. "Yes, it will, Papa."

Yet her gaze lifted to the sky in search of the gray clouds that would signal impending moisture. She found none. Not even a wisp. Only a deep and perfect azure that seemed to go on forever.

Unexpected unease fluttered in her belly. The rain *had* to come. If it didn't, the sheep wouldn't thrive, and then they'd produce a coarser wool, not the silky fleece which would fetch a higher price at market.

Papa took great pride in his flock, which bore the prized Merino bloodline known for their fine, thick coats. Only a few more weeks, and then *finally*, Zurina could have the house she had long dreamed of. Papa had promised. The house that would give her the respect she craved.

If only Mama could have the house, too.

Sadness tore into Zurina's heart, but she resisted its pain. Mama was gone, and Mikolas was, too. Not dead, but *gone,* and she had no idea where. She only had Papa, and she would take care of him as he deserved.

"Maybe it will not hurt to stay here," her father muttered in resignation. "Maybe he will not see."

His dark head angled, as if he searched into the

distance, somewhere past Sun River and onto land where Zurina had never been, seeking assurance that they were doing the right thing.

That they would be safe.

Their rig rolled to a slow halt, and she realized... he was afraid of Trey Wells.

Her lip curled.

Though Papa had spoken of him often enough, Zurina had never met the man, but she chafed against his power. The unfairness of it. She cursed his ability to strike fear into her father who thought of him first and the flocks second. She despised both Wells men, and every cattleman like them, whose arrogance and erroneous beliefs denied the sheepmen their rights to use the land and its water for the same reasons they claimed them for themselves.

To survive.

"I don't care if he sees us, Papa." She tossed her head with a haughty sniff. "He doesn't control us. We owe him nothing."

Her father grunted and swung out of the wagon seat, down onto the ground. For a moment, he didn't move, as if he waited for his tired muscles to loosen. "He has been generous with us, 'Rina."

"So you say." Her father's weariness tugged at her. The years of sheepherding that had begun to seep into his bones. Or maybe it was the grief from losing Mama that clawed at him, making him hurt.

She resisted his logic, driven from the agreement

he'd honored for so many months. She forced a consoling smile onto her lips.

"Then he shouldn't mind if we aren't in the valley tonight, eh?" she added sweetly.

He heaved a heavy sigh and shook his head. Zurina couldn't tell if he was exasperated with her. Or merely amused. He waggled a finger at her. "You would be wise not to cross him, daughter. You do not know what he is capable of."

His warning reminded her she couldn't forget what Sutton Wells had done. And that blood always ran deep. Her smile faded.

Did Papa know something about Trey Wells that he wasn't telling her? Did he harbor a secret like Mama had for so many years?

"But, we are here, and here we will stay." Papa's expression revealed his misgivings. "It will be dark soon. Get a fire going in the stove, 'Rina, and start our supper. I will take care of the sheep."

Zurina's gaze lingered over him as he shuffled toward the herd, calling out to his faithful companion, Gorri, the Australian shepherd he'd raised from a pup.

And I will take care of you, Papa.

She kept the vow to herself. He was accustomed to living a solitary existence for weeks on end while he tended the flock. Except for those occasions when Mama and Zurina rode out to see him, he took care of himself. He wouldn't think he needed her.

But he did. Zurina refused to let him forget they were a family, and they needed each other.

She dismounted, and the feel of the lush grass beneath her feet told her she'd made the right decision in convincing him to leave Sun River Valley. Striding to the back of the wagon, she tugged open the door and climbed inside, just like she had so often before.

Except now she paused, not from the stuffy heat that assailed her, but from the sheer smallness of the area her father called home for too many months out of the year.

It was as if she was seeing his quarters for the first time. The sheep wagon was a marvel of efficiency, with its bunk built neatly beneath the window, and cabinets below that. In between, a pull-out table, and along the sides of the wagon, a pair of wooden benches, with drawers for added storage. A couple of lanterns hung from the hickory ribs which held the layers of canvas strapped tight over them. A stove near the back door aided cooking and provided warmth.

Efficiency. For Papa, it was enough.

But not for Zurina. She wanted more for him. For both of them. A house with rooms and furniture and pretty curtains. A house with enough space to raise children. A house in which to love a husband and grow old with him—

She stiffened.

What were these thoughts about a *husband?* Since

her mother's death, and Mikolas's leaving, Zurina had squelched her need for one. Her innermost desire for a man to call her own. She had Papa to think of. She had to take care of him, keep him from being lonely. She had to fight the hurt and rage from what Sutton Wells had done.

They must heal together.

In a few resolved steps, Zurina strode to the window and yanked it wide. A breeze blew, sucked inward by the open back door and carrying the thick air right out through it. She plopped a can of corn on the bench, then added one of tomatoes with actions brisk and snappish and driven by the sour mood which had suddenly gripped her.

The *husband* thoughts. She hadn't had them of late, not so much since Mama died, anyway, and why did she have to have them rush back now?

She pulled an iron skillet from the drawer and set it on the stove with a noisy thump. Her thinking freshened her determination not to live the life her mother had. A paltry existence with a sheepherder who left her alone, night after night after night.

Zurina refused to be lonely.

Except…she already was.

Lonely for a husband.

Hating her weakness, she set her teeth and dropped a slab of salt pork into the pan, then reached for a box of matches. Before she could strike one, Gorri's persistent barking reached through the open window and clawed for her attention.

The barking wasn't his usual, like when he herded the sheep, and her distracted glance shifted to the window, lighting onto her father first as he walked amongst the flock. He halted at the dog's yapping and turned; his dark head swiveled toward the wagon.

Someone, or something, was outside.

For one wild moment, Zurina thought of her brother. Mikolas. That he'd come back, after all these tortuous weeks, repentant and no longer angry.

A horse snuffled, and the hope surged through her. She dropped the matches and leaped toward the back door.

Then froze.

It wasn't her brother riding in. Zurina didn't recognize the horse, but she knew the breed. A quarter horse. Thoroughbred. Finer than any Basque would own.

And in the saddle, looking elegant in mourning black, the most beautiful woman she had ever seen.

Chapter Two

~~~~~

She didn't notice Zurina at first, but instead channeled her stare at Gorri, as if his swift approach intimidated her. Her dark skirts draped the horse's sides, and the toes of her patent leather shoes peeked out from the stirrups. A feathered hat perched on her head, and she carried herself in the saddle with a regal grace that held Zurina fascinated.

The quarter horse pranced, but the woman held him in line with ease, revealing she was an accomplished equestrian, too. Yet her quick inhalation indicated a surge of alarm the closer Gorri drew.

Zurina jerked her glance toward the dog and spoke sharply in Basque. Gorri immediately halted a few yards away, but his stiff-legged stance remained watchful, warning their visitor he'd allow no trouble.

Zurina turned back to the woman. Something kept Zurina in the wagon's doorway, an inner reluctance, perhaps, to have the woman look down at her while seated on the horse.

"He won't hurt you," she said.

"Oh, my." The woman pressed a hand to her bosom. "He looks vicious. He gave me a fright."

Her fingers appeared pale and smooth against her black dress. On one finger, a ruby ring sat beneath the knuckle.

"He isn't vicious." Zurina dragged her gaze off the jewel and tried not to think what a stone like that would cost. "It's just that we don't often see strangers out here."

"Yes, well, I'm lost, I'm afraid." Her chin trembled, and she glanced away.

Clearly she was on the brink of tears, and sympathy welled in Zurina.

"I'm sorry you're lost," she said gently. "Where were you going?"

"Great Falls."

"Oh. I see."

Zurina didn't have the heart to tell the poor woman how far she'd drifted off course. That the main road leading into the city was several miles in the opposite direction.

"You cannot go there tonight."

Papa's gruff voice startled their visitor, and

her black-hatted head whipped toward him. "Excuse me?"

He halted near Gorri and set his thick hands on his hips. "The sun will set soon. You must stop for the night."

"But—"

"You cannot ride in the dark, a woman alone."

Her glance jumped to Zurina, then back to Papa. "But it's not dark yet. If you merely show me the way back to the main road—"

Papa shook his head. "We are too far from the road. The sun will be gone before I can take you there."

Her chin quivered again. "Then what am I to do?"

"You will stay here." Though kindly, Papa's tone sounded firm. "You can sleep in the wagon with 'Rina. I will stay outside."

"What?" She gaped at him. "Stay here? With you? Why, I don't even *know* you!"

She sounded so horrified, Zurina couldn't help a tiny flare of resentment.

"We don't know you, either," she said coolly. "But still we extend the kindness."

"I am Gabirel Vasco." Papa held out a grubby hand. "This is my daughter, Zurina."

Again, the woman's gaze bounced between them. "You're sheepherders, aren't you?"

Zurina stiffened. The implication of what she

meant but didn't say stung as sharply as if the woman had swung outward and slapped their cheeks.

But Papa merely nodded. "Yes. The sheep are ours."

She lifted a trembling hand to her lips. "I can't do it."

"What?"

Her spine flattened, and her chin kicked upward. "My name is Allethaire Gibson. I'm engaged to be married to Trey Wells. Perhaps you've heard of him?"

Papa instantly blanched.

Zurina's world tilted.

Of all the men this woman, this Allethaire, might've named...but of *course* Trey would marry a woman like her. Beautiful, wealthy—and bred with a cattleman's thinking.

"We've heard of him," Zurina gritted.

"Well, he simply wouldn't want me staying here with—with—well—"

"Mutton-punchers?" Zurina's brow arched in sarcasm.

The other's lips curled downward. "Yes. Or whatever else you call yourselves."

Zurina drew herself up and was suddenly very glad she hadn't left the wagon after all. "Then perhaps if you ride very fast away from here, you could make it to—"

"Zurina!" Her father's black eyes sparked with censure for her rudeness.

Her nostrils flared, but she said nothing more.

Looking miserable, Papa took hold of the horse's bridle. "Come down from the saddle, miss. Zurina has just begun our supper. You will feel better when you eat."

For a moment, Allethaire didn't move, as if she had to drudge up the will to comply. Finally she dismounted. Swayed. And only steadied herself with the hasty assistance of Papa's hand upon her elbow.

She pulled from his grasp, as if she disliked the feel of it. "I won't be here long, you know."

"No. Not long."

His veiled glance met Zurina's, and she shot him a look that revealed her annoyance at being forced to give the ungrateful Allethaire Gibson their hospitality, Trey Wells be damned. Papa's glance in turn responded they had no choice, because now Trey was sure to learn of their illicit presence on his range, that they weren't in the valley where they belonged, and what was going to happen *now*?

Papa led the quarter horse toward the river, where he would hobble him with their own for the night. He walked with shoulders hunched, as if the world weighed heavy upon them, and her heart ached at the sight.

Her rebellion withered.

Because of the sheep, they could do nothing to

upset the fragile Allethaire further, and Zurina vowed to be more hospitable to the woman.

A *cattleman's* woman.

She shifted her glance, just as Allethaire capped a small leather flask and wiped her mouth with the back of her hand. She stood with her back half-twisted from view, as if she tried to hide what she was doing but couldn't help herself.

Liquid courage.

She stuffed the flask into her handbag, turned to face Zurina with eyes glazed and cheeks flushed… and hiccupped.

Zurina refrained from groaning out loud. Allethaire Gibson was in no shape to go anywhere drunk, and with a growing, sinking feeling, Zurina began to realize that all along, Papa had been right.

They never should have left Sun River Valley.

"How could anyone live in here?" Allethaire asked. She stood in the doorway and peered into the wagon as if it were some mysterious black hole that would swallow her up if she drew any closer. "It's ungodly small."

Zurina stabbed a piece of salt pork sizzling in the skillet. She shouldn't have been annoyed by the comment; she'd thought the same thing herself only a short time ago. But a wave of defensiveness for her father's home, his very manner of living, swept through her, and she schooled her features to keep the irritation from showing.

She even managed a smile. "Small, yes, but it's quite comfortable."

"If one was a mouse, I suppose."

Zurina's smile disappeared, and she dropped the meat onto the plate, added a sloppy spoonful of corn, another of tomatoes then thrust the whole thing toward Allethaire.

"That would be a matter of opinion, I think," she said, offended.

But Allethaire didn't seem to hear. Her glance lowered toward the plate. "What's this?"

"Your supper."

Her glance lifted again, this time with her jaw jutted at an impertinent angle. "I'm not hungry."

"No?" Zurina withdrew the meal. "Fine."

She set the plate on the table with a clatter and drew in a calming breath. She reminded herself Allethaire was engaged to Trey Wells, and anything she and Papa did tonight would surely find its way back to him. If Allethaire felt they treated her poorly and told him so, what would he do?

Ban them forever from Sun River Valley?

Allethaire was accustomed to the best in life. Beef instead of salt pork. China instead of a dented tin plate. Pristine tablecloths, glistening silver, formal dining rooms.

Well, she'd get none of those things now.

"I'm not staying here," Allethaire muttered.

Despite her words, however, she took an unsteady step into the wagon and dropped onto the bench, a half-moment after Zurina scooped up a bundle of month-old newspapers to make room. She'd brought them for her father to help fill his time, knowing he'd read each one from front page to last, then read them all over again until she brought him more.

Zurina lit the lantern to ward off the deepening dusk and reached for another plate.

"It's too late to ride into Great Falls," she said slowly, as if she were speaking to a child who refused to comprehend the obvious.

But Allethaire impatiently waved a hand. "No, no. You don't understand. I'm not staying in Montana."

"Oh?"

"I'm going home."

"Great Falls is not your home?"

"My home is in *Minnesota*."

"I see."

Except Zurina didn't see. Not really. And what business was it of hers where the woman lived?

"He'll know I meant what I said when he learns I'm gone." Again, that chin quivered. The faint scent of brandy hovered in the air. "It'll serve him right to face the scandal of my leaving him."

Sympathy pulled at Zurina. It seemed the spirits had loosened Allethaire's tongue. Whatever the reasoning for her petulance, she felt it deeply.

"You mean Trey Wells?" Zurina dared to ask.

"He's so damned stubborn. Pardon my language." Her head swung, and she glared at the window, as if she envisioned him in the glass. "I told him he must choose. His stupid ranch—or me."

Well. Clearly the man had some serious problems with his intended. Zurina found herself at a loss for words. Perhaps Allethaire was being difficult in her demands and expectations. Or maybe Trey was.

Allethaire's glance swiveled back toward her. "His father is dead now."

"Dead?" The news rocked through Zurina. "Sutton Wells?"

"He was murdered three days ago."

Zurina pressed her fingers to her lips in horror.

"There's not a better time than now for Trey to leave Montana and start over with me in Minnesota." Allethaire's chin jutted stubbornly.

Sutton Wells was dead. *Murdered.* Zurina could hardly fathom the implications. For Papa and herself. For Trey Wells. But mostly for Mikolas…

Her father appeared in the narrow doorway, and she swung toward him on a jumble of distracted thoughts. Papa dipped his head, stepped inward and the wagon turned smaller than ever.

As if she only now took the time to study him more thoroughly, Allethaire's glance lowered. And lowered. Until her scrutiny could go no further than his worn leather shoes.

Which only made Zurina keenly aware of the patches on his trousers. Of his thin shirt with the sleeves torn short above the elbows. Of his tattered cap and his dire need of a haircut.

Allethaire wouldn't understand why the sheep-herder placed little importance on his appearance. Who would he impress but the sheep?

"A couple of riders are coming," he said. "Make sure you have enough food to feed them, Zurina."

"Who is coming?" she demanded in surprise, hearing Gorri's barking. She couldn't remember having had so many visitors before.

She fixed her gaze on the window and found the silhouetted shapes of a pair of cowboys riding off a low ridge. In light of Gorri's agitated warnings, they skirted the sheep but kept their attention on them.

"Is it Trey?" Allethaire asked, jumping to her feet and peering out the window, too.

"Maybe," Papa said, clearly uneasy. "Or maybe they are his men, out looking for you."

She swung around. "Don't tell them I'm here, do you understand?"

Her father appeared taken aback. "How can I not?"

"There's no place for you to hide, Allethaire," Zurina said firmly. She refused to play the woman's selfish game. "They would only need to look into the wagon to see you."

The cowboys had moved out of the window's

range. Hoofbeats sounded louder. So did Gorri's barking. Papa pivoted toward the door.

"We cannot have trouble tonight," he said, his voice firm, yet Zurina detected a vein of pleading, too. "It is important that we do not."

"I should never have let you talk me into staying with you." Allethaire glowered at him in the lantern light. "I could be halfway to Great Falls by now."

Resentment flared within Zurina. The woman had only to look outside to see how dark it was getting. Had she imbibed so much brandy that she couldn't understand staying in their camp was for her own safety?

"Oh?" Zurina couldn't veil her exasperation. "Perhaps those cowboys out there could—"

A gunshot exploded.

She jerked.

Allethaire gasped.

And for a moment…the world stood still.

In the next, chaos erupted. The realization that Gorri's bark had turned into a single shrill yelp. That his furry body rolled past. That her father let out an enraged yell and jumped to the outside. That a man on horseback suddenly loomed, reached out with a snarl and yanked him forward.

Zurina couldn't move. Couldn't comprehend what was happening.

Then, a sudden fear for her father raced through her chest. She threw aside the plate she'd been filling and leaped toward the door. She couldn't fathom why anyone would want to hurt Gabirel Vasco, or Gorri, and oh, God—

She landed on the ground without benefit of steps. Seeing her father struggling against the cowboy's grasp, that the man had his hand upraised, a revolver in his gloved fist, a new round of horror slammed into her.

"Leave him alone!" she shouted. "Stop!"

But the butt of the revolver whipped across her father's jaw, and he hurtled into the dirt. Moaned. And went still.

Anguish tore through Zurina. She fell to her knees beside him with a sob.

"I ain't kin to lamb-lickers," the cowboy spat.

She twisted toward him. Fury for what he'd done, and why, shot through her blood.

"Leave us alone," she snapped.

He wore a bandanna high over his face; in the dusk, his sooty eyes shone hard with contempt. The shadows worked against her—she couldn't get a good look at him, but in all her life, she'd never known anyone so vile, so cold-blooded.

"Anyone else in that wagon?" he demanded.

Papa stirred and lifted one knee, as if he tried to get up but couldn't. He muttered something unintelligible. Zurina didn't have to hear his words to know what he wanted her to say.

That she had to do what she could to protect Trey Wells's woman.

Yet, what did they owe her? Or him? A cattleman who inspired fear and trepidation in her father? A man who helped himself to untold acres of the massive range while sharing with Gabirel Vasco only a tiny piece of it?

A match hissed. "I asked you a question, honey. Anyone else in that wagon?"

She needed all her willpower not to steal a glance at the doorway. Instinct told her Allethaire wouldn't be standing there anyway, visible in the lantern light. She'd want to remain unseen. Zurina envisioned her cowering, determined to keep Trey Wells, her intended husband, and any of his men from finding out she was there.

"No," she grated. "There is no one."

The masked cowboy turned toward his accomplice and jerked his chin in silent command. The second man produced a long, strong, ominous stick.

A club.

Zurina died a little inside.

She stood. Slowly. The terror built in her. Cold, cloying. Choking against her heart, her throat, making it hard to breathe. A terror from the very real certainty of what the two cowboys intended to do.

"Please," she said. Never before had she begged,

but she was prepared to do so now. On her knees if she must. "Please do not do this."

As if she'd never spoken, the other man withdrew a revolver from his holster, turned and broke into an easy lope toward the flock. A group of ewes had strayed from the rest, their heads low toward the grass. He leveled his arm, fired, and one dropped. He swung the club against another, and she fell, too.

Deep and blistering agony seared Zurina, and she screamed in rage. Her sheep. Dear God, her precious sheep, and before she could think to stop herself, before she could comprehend the danger, she began to run toward the distant stranger, compelled by a burgeoning hate for him and her rising desperation to stop the slaughter. To save her dreams and that of her father's, because without the flock, they had nothing. They had *nothing*.

"Stop it! Stop it!" she cried. "Stop!"

Another gunshot rang out, this time from behind her. From the man who'd assaulted Papa and started this nightmare. In the next instant, glass shattered— the lantern inside the wagon—and she swung back around, just as an explosive *whoosh* ripped the air.

Flames leaped from the doorway and shot the darkness with blinding color. Her fingers flew to her mouth in a new wave of horror.

Allethaire!

She was still inside, still hiding, and Zurina raced back toward the wagon.

"Allethaire! Allethaire!" she shouted.

In his need to get to Allethaire, to help her, Zurina's father heaved himself to a standing position and staggered toward the doorway. Allethaire appeared in the glow of the flames with her arm flung upward to protect her face, her skirts gathered close to her body.

"Jump out!" Papa called.

"Hurry!" Zurina urged, reaching them, fearing the stove could explode, too. "Now, Allethaire!"

Shrieking, the woman took a flying leap to the ground. Instinctively Zurina held out her arms, half-catching her. The impetus of the jump nearly knocked her to the ground.

"Allethaire?" Unexpectedly the masked cowboy spoke her name sharply. "Allethaire Gibson?"

She twisted toward him with a gasp, righting her hat when it went askew. "Yes!"

"Don't say anything to him." Zurina pulled her away from the heat of the flames, her mind racing on how they could save the wagon. Save themselves. And poor Gorri, who she didn't know was alive or dead.

"You're Trey Wells's woman, ain't you?"

"I don't know you." Allethaire stood a little straighter, as if she considered it her right to be above him, though his seat on the horse forced her to tilt her head back. "Are you one of his outfit?" she demanded.

The cowboy urged his horse closer, step by step, stalking Allethaire. Stalking Zurina, too.

Over the snap of the fiery flames, gunshots popped in the distance. Into the flock. Again and again.

"Leave us alone," Zurina said, hating him. Hating the break in her voice, the despair she tried to hide. "Have you not done enough?"

The bandanna-wrapped face swiveled toward her. "It'll stop, honey. Just give her to me."

Zurina's step faltered. An ugly, menacing dread flickered inside her. "What?"

"Allethaire. Hand her over."

He was close, so close. Only an arm's length separated them. He had only to bend down, reach out…

"What are you talking about?" Allethaire snapped, stopping in midstride in a burst of ill-timed defiance.

Zurina tugged at her, to keep her moving. Deeper into the dark.

"'Rina, we must run from him." Papa's arm slipped around her shoulders, a feeble attempt at protecting her, urging them all to flee. He spoke in Basque, his voice an unsteady whisper in her ear.

But Zurina knew he couldn't protect them. They couldn't run. Not from the gun. Or the man on the horse. Not from anything. Not anymore.

It was too late, too late, too late.

She tasted her father's fear, for it matched her own. The fear every sheepman endured from the men who despised them. The cattlemen who would always despise them.

"Might be he'll do a little bargaining for her," the cowboy said, his voice soft, amused, eerily muffled through the bandanna.

"No," Zurina said. Her arm tightened on Allethaire. Allethaire tightened her grip back. "Leave us alone."

"We'll kill those maggots of yours. Every damned one." The revolver waved. "You don't want us to do that, do you?"

Flames roared higher into the black sky. A sob welled up in Zurina's throat.

"'Rina." Papa's voice quavered with grief. With uncertainty.

"You'll never get away with—with hurting me," Allethaire said. "Trey, he'll kill you for this. He'll—"

Suddenly the revolver swung to the side, toward Papa and a shot rang out. He grunted, spun and fell to the ground.

Zurina screamed and whirled toward him; her grasp dropped from Allethaire to reach for her father.

The cowboy leaned down and snatched Allethaire's arm with a vicious strength none of them could have foreseen. In one cruel swipe, he backhanded her across the face, caught her as she crumpled and hauled her limp body onto his horse.

Zurina pivoted in horror, torn from helping her father, torn in knowing she must save Allethaire, but the cowboy spurred his horse away, toward the glow of the firelight. The horse's flanks gleamed, and in a single blink, she glimpsed the brand burned into the hide.

And then, Allethaire was gone.

Chapter Three

Trey reined in on the crest of a low ridge, narrowed an eye and contemplated what he saw.

Sheep scattered along this side of Sun River. Some herdsman had broken range rules and driven his flock onto Wells land. Wasn't normal how spread out the woollies were, some on their feet, some on the ground. Wasn't normal how quiet they were, either. Anyone would expect to hear plenty of that damned bleating. Where were the dogs that always guarded them?

Trey took a slow sip of coffee gone cold and told himself he had worse problems to contemplate.

"What do you make of it?" Nubby asked, running a frowning glance around him.

Trey tossed aside the last dregs of coffee,

twisted in the saddle and stuffed the tin cup into the leather bag.

"Not sure," he said finally, straightening. "But we have to keep moving."

He nudged his horse forward. Nubby did the same. Both of them, drawing closer to the sheep.

"So quiet around here you can just about hear daylight coming," Nubby said in a hushed tone.

Trey grunted. The sun had barely cracked over the horizon. They'd only come this way in case Allethaire had gotten lost and decided to follow the river to help find her way.

But they'd found no sign of her yet. Not a one.

Trey's thoughts fell back to yesterday, when he'd ridden into Great Falls and went straight to her hotel, only to learn she hadn't returned—her empty room proved she hadn't. A demanding confrontation with the hotel's staff confirmed her absence, and he'd hurried back to the ranch as fast as hell could scorch a feather, roused Nubby from his bed and set out again.

If Trey didn't find her soon, he'd have to round up a posse to help. And no telling what her father was doing. Hell, Paris would likely demand the governor of Montana Territory call up the United States Army and get them involved....

Trey shook his head at the trouble she'd caused. Had he ever known a more thoughtless female?

After riding all night and into the dawn, burdened

with worry for Allethaire, he didn't want to deal with the troublesome foreboding he was feeling now. Over a flock of worthless sheep. He had no time for it.

"Hell, Trey. Look."

The cowboy pointed, and Trey's glance dropped to a lamb sleeping on the ground. The sound of horse hooves tromping over range grass should've alerted the young animal they were near.

But it didn't.

The bloated body explained why. So did the blood trickling out of one ear. Trey's sense of foreboding hiked up a good-sized notch. The lamb was sleeping all right. For good.

"Been clubbed to death," Nubby said. "Look how swelled up he is."

"They all are."

They continued in a slow walk, deeper into the flock, their scrutiny clawing the ground. Ewes and rams littered the grass. The cowboy pointed again. And again.

"This one's been shot. So has this one," he said.

Trey's gaze lifted to sweep the range in slow, thorough perusal. In the rising light from dawn, dark crimson stained the thick, wool coats of sheep numbered more than he could fairly count. The heavy silence, eerie from death, hung in the air.

"It's a full-fledged massacre," he muttered.

In unison, both halted. Nubby didn't need to say the words Trey knew he was thinking.

Where was the sheepherder who'd been guarding the flock? Or his dog?

Were they dead, too?

Trey detected a faint scent of wood burning, and he searched for a campfire. He failed to find one, but his stare lingered over something black in the distance. Something smoldering.

Trey's mind conjectured what that something was, and his foreboding twisted deeper. He reached for his Smith & Wesson, tucked in its holster. Nubby reached for his, too.

Without speaking, they nudged their mounts forward once again. Toward that blackened shape. Trey kept his stare on the burned-out wagon; Nubby couldn't seem to keep his off the masses of bloated, slaughtered sheep.

"Would've been time to shear 'em soon," he said. "They're full-wooled as can be."

Trey had little tolerance for the woollybacks. They were prickly thorns in the hides of every cattleman. They poisoned the range and drank water holes dry, but no stockman—even one who raised sheep— deserved to have his herd wiped out.

That this one was near ready for market only made the loss worse. Much worse.

He could hardly fathom what could've instigated the violence. Or where the killers might be. If they'd escaped. Or if they were in hiding—watching, waiting, while Trey and Nubby rode closer.

The uncertainty heightened Trey's senses, and he braced himself to expect the unexpected. The horses stepped around the four-legged mounds with a careful, ginger tread. Ominous and suffocating, the silence weighed on him, and the closer they drew, the more the air turned heavy with the acrid scent of death, smoke and charred wood.

Suddenly the hairs on the back of his neck rose. An instinctive warning he'd long ago learned to trust, and his finger moved over the revolver's trigger. His muscles coiled, one by one. His heart drummed a slow, methodical beat—

Thwap!

A bullet hit the ground in front of him, throwing dirt, and his startled horse reared. Teeth clenched against an oath, Trey gripped the reins to keep his seat; his gaze jerked toward the ringing sound of the gunshot while his body readied to feel the burn of a second, better-aimed bullet.

Movement stirred around the smoldering wagon, and a woman appeared. Trey abruptly drew up. And stared.

"Damn," Nubby grated under his breath. "Either she's a lousy shot or she's just playing with us."

Trey kept his eye on her. She stood with an aging Henry rifle pressed to her shoulder, her sandaled feet spread in a stance that declared she'd shoot whenever she caught the inkling. Her hair flowed long and tangled down one arm, the strands as dark and thick as the crescents of her lashes. Her slim body and olive skin declared her Basque heritage, but it was the haunted look in her fierce expression that moved something deep inside Trey's chest.

"Don't come any closer," she commanded. "I have two bullets left. One for each of you."

Despite the harshness of her words, her voice slid as smooth as warm honey to his ears. He would've been intrigued with the way she talked, each word laced with the exotic lilt of her people, if she wasn't so hell-bent on burning some powder on them.

"Looks like you had some trouble here, ma'am," he said carefully, not moving. "What happened?"

A tremble went through her, so slight he might've imagined it. But he *didn't* imagine it, and a grudging admiration for her bravado built inside him.

"Get out of here," she snapped.

His eye narrowed. "You can use some help out here."

She made a sound of contempt. "Do you think I'm so stupid that I'd believe you?"

Her response left him scrambling to comprehend why she *wouldn't* believe him. Did she think she could manage this carnage? A woman alone? And why would she want to?

"Someone set out to hurt you," he said.

"Go away." Pain flashed across her features. As if she willed herself to triumph over it, she drew in a deep breath. "Now."

"Reckon she's not feeling hospitable since we got two barrels trained on her," Nubby muttered under his breath.

In the distraction of being shot at, by a female no less, Trey had forgotten that little detail, and he immediately sheathed his Smith & Wesson.

"Put your hands up, Nub," Trey said, his voice low between them. His guard never wavered from the woman. "She'll feel better for it."

The cowboy obeyed and showed her his palms. "Let's hope."

Her glance jumped between them. If she was relieved by their actions, she didn't show it.

"Very good," she said. The end of the rifle jerked. "Now it's easy for you to ride away. Both of you, go."

"We're not going anywhere."

Trey held her black-eyed glance, and an unexpected zing of awareness slid through his blood. Distracting him. Leaving him feeling slightly off-kilter.

That she managed to have the effect on him rankled when she was a hair-trigger away from shooting him dead.

"I'm going to ask you again," he said in a low voice. "Are you hurt?"

"No."

He conceded she didn't appear to be. "Anyone else out here with you?"

For a fraction, the *barest* of fractions, her gaze wavered. "No."

"You're alone?"

"Yes."

Beside him, Nubby grunted his surprise. Trey admitted skepticism and a growing conviction her quick, curt responses were lies. For all his time living on the Montana range, he'd never heard of a woman herding a flock of sheep on her own.

He would have.

"Who did this to you?" he demanded. "To your sheep?"

This time, her chin hardened, and her eyes flashed with hate. "I don't know."

But she did know. Something. And he'd had enough of her game. He straightened, swung a leg over the cantle and dropped to the ground.

Introducing themselves would be the first step in getting her to trust them. He intended to peel away her lies to find the truth underneath of what really happened to her sheep.

He crooked a thumb toward Nubby. "This is Nubby Thomas. He works for me over at the Wells Cattle Company."

Her breath hitched. The Henry sagged a few inches.

"And my name is Trey Wells," he said.

She paled. Swayed. "You are…him?"

He nodded. Once. Considering she had a bad

case of trigger itch, he kept close watch on her rifle.
"I am."

Her lip curled. *"Damn you."*

Then, before he could even think it, she snarled, jerked the gun back up to her shoulder and fired.

She should have killed the bastard.

But something compelled Zurina to save his worthless life and give him a scare he wouldn't forget. She aimed the bullet close.

But not as close as she wanted.

The lead plug winged its way over his shoulder. Past his ear. He choked out an oath and leaped sideways. When she didn't fire again, he slammed his gaze into hers.

"Now you only have one bullet left, woman. Unless you're lying about that, too."

She wasn't, but she had no intention of telling him so. Let him wonder. Let him worry. He'd caused her enough of both of late.

Still, his perception unnerved her. He knew she wasn't alone. She had to stay vigilant, or he'd be quick to take advantage.

For all his faults, Zurina never expected such blatant deception from Trey Wells. He acted as if he knew nothing about the attack on Vasco sheep. And this concern for her he showed—pah! It only proved yet again how devious he was.

She couldn't trust him. Not past the blink of her eye.

"Next time, I won't miss putting a hole in your heart, Mr. Wells," she said coldly. "One bullet is all I'd need."

"Now listen here, ma'am."

Her glance jumped to the other cowboy. Nubby Thomas. Gray-haired and wiry, his hands still in the air, he appeared more compassionate than vindictive, but she refused to fall for the ploy. He rode with Trey Wells, didn't he? He couldn't be trusted, either.

"We're here to help, that's all," he continued, frowning at her. "Looks like you could use it."

A sudden lump jumped into her throat. Help? Even if it were true that is what they wanted to do, they were too late. No one could help her or Papa. Not anymore.

"So why don't you just put down that shootin' iron, young lady, and we'll get to the bottom of what happened out here," Nubby finished.

Her old Henry remained leveled at Trey Wells's chest, but she kept the gray-haired cowboy in her sights. Watched as he slowly, carefully, dismounted from his horse.

Now, both men were on the ground. Only a half dozen yards away. And an image of Allethaire, kicking and shrieking as she was being taken against her will, shot through Zurina's memory.

She wasn't so foolish to think she could fight both

these men if they rushed forward and grabbed her, and a ripple of apprehension, of very real fear of the possibility of being attacked, shuddered through her. She bettered her stance and took strands of comfort in the one bullet she had left to defend herself.

"I don't believe you mean what you say," she said as bravely as she could. "I will tell you again. Leave us or I will shoot."

Nubby's hands lowered, and he slid a glance at Trey. Whose mouth moved into a sardonic, triumphant quirk.

"'Us'?" he asked softly.

Too late, she realized her mistake.

"I include the sheep," she said, scrambling to rectify the blunder. She even managed to infuse a convincing firmness into the words.

"There's someone else here with you," he said sharply. "Who?"

"And where?" Nubby demanded right after.

"There is no one but me—"

"'Rina. Please. Enough of this.'"

She started at the sound of her father's voice, and she could no more keep from swiveling toward him than she could keep herself from breathing. Her heart tilted at how pale he looked in the morning sun. How weak. He leaned heavily on his uninjured arm, and though he braced himself on the blackened wagon frame, he appeared ready to fall at any moment.

An inadvertent sound of dismay slipped from her

throat. She'd given him strict orders to stay hidden beneath the pile of pine branches she'd gathered and piled near the wagon. A crude attempt to stay warm, to be safe. To get themselves through the awful night—and the inevitable confrontation with these men.

But before she could go to him, the rifle was suddenly wrenched from her grasp, and she stumbled forward from the force. Trey Wells loomed in front of her, with a scowl as fierce as thunder, and who did he think he was, taking away the one piece of defense against him she had left?

Hadn't he taken enough from her already?

With a cry of rebellion and unbridled fury, she lunged toward him and latched both hands onto the old Henry, one on the barrel, the other on the butt, and tugged. Hard.

"Give it back, damn you," she snapped.

"Not a chance, sweetheart," he growled, and tugged right back. Harder.

She fell against him. Thigh to thigh, hip to hip, with the rifle wedged between them.

Through the thin layers of her skirt, the strength in those denim-clad thighs branded themselves against hers. The buckle of his gun belt pressed into her abdomen, but she refused to be intimidated. She had no patience in being afraid.

But she couldn't help being aware. Of Trey Wells

as a man. His power. His control. That he could easily overpower her, right here.

Now.

His scent surrounded her—leather, horse, coffee. Man. But it was his gaze that held her in its clutches, as if he wove some bizarre spell over her, holding her against her will. Making her feel as if she could drown in the glittering bronze depths of his shadowed gaze.

The planes of his face shown harsh above her. Tiny creases etched the corners of his eyes. The sun had tanned his skin and rough bristle covered his cheeks, giving him the look of the lawless.

A look that suited him. Trey Wells had no law— except for his own. He'd victimized her and destroyed her because of his arrogance and superiority over the sheepman.

God, she hated him.

But she hated his effect on her even more, and in a determined burst of rebellion, she tugged on the rifle again.

To no avail.

"Leave us alone," she hissed. "You've taken what you want from us, haven't you?"

He speared her with a dark glower. "Think whatever you want of me, but you need help, woman, and I'll be giving it to you."

As if to prove his point, he swiftly jerked his arms upward and yanked the rifle from her grasp.

She gave up fighting him and leveled him with a fierce glower of her own. "How kind of you."

"'Rina," her father said, his tone raspy. Wheezy. "Do not argue with him. Have you forgotten who he is?"

Her nostrils flared with disdain. "I have not forgotten, Papa. How could I ever forget?"

"He is…*Trey Wells.*"

Alarmed by the wheezing sound which threaded his words, she stepped toward him, but before she got there, before she could help, her father's knees buckled, he crumpled to the ground and went still.

Chapter Four

She feared he was dead.

But, dear God in heaven, the faint pulse at his wrist assured her he wasn't. Blinking back tears of anguish, of immense relief, she bent over him and kissed his cheek, whispering her love and assurances she would do all she could to make things right for them again.

"He needs a doctor."

Zurina took a moment to compose herself, then sat back on her heels and speared Trey Wells with a condescending glance. He squatted on his haunches across from her, his expression grave. Did he think she was blind to all her father had suffered?

"I know," she said coldly.

"He's lost a lot of blood."

She refused to look down at Papa's crimson-stained shirt, which still glistened wet against his shoulder. "I know that, too."

The anguish inside her roiled deeper, and she hovered on the edge of losing her composure again. She took Papa's limp hand into both of hers and held on.

"I did all I could for him," she said stiffly. "But I had nothing. I—everything we had was in the wagon, and everything was burned, and—"

She stopped herself from rambling and drew in a breath. What did Trey Wells care what she had lost—her wagon, its contents or otherwise? Certainly he had no care for her sheep. He would *want* so many to die.

Somber, Trey carefully parted Papa's thin cotton shirt and peered beneath to inspect the wound. "How many times was he hit?"

In her mind, Zurina could still hear the blast of the masked cowboy's gun. Could still see her father spin and fall with a dull thud to the ground.

"Once," she said, swallowing.

Trey drew back. "Nowhere else besides the shoulder?"

"No."

She'd fashioned a bandage, but it was crude at best, and from the way the wound seeped blood, ineffectual.

"The bullet still in him?"

"Yes. I couldn't see that it came out, so yes, it must still be in his shoulder."

Knowing what must happen, what lay ahead, she squeezed her father's hand tighter.

"Got to come out," Trey said.

"He needs a surgeon, yes."

"A surgeon." He regarded her. "You see one out here?"

In spite of his sarcasm, her glance lifted to the range sprawling beyond the horizon. If only a trained physician would suddenly appear. Or a magician, who could magically wave his wand and make Papa strong again.

"Of course not," she said.

"We need to remove the damn thing. Now. Before he gets any sicker."

Zurina took a moment to comprehend his intentions. After what had happened, after the terrible slaughter of the sheep, Trey Wells wanted to help?

Why?

Who was he trying to fool?

Nubby Thomas strode forward. He'd taken her rifle and tied it to his saddle for safekeeping, leaving Trey free to examine her father without reprisal.

"I've got some rotgut to give him, ma'am, if it'll make you feel any better about it." Nubby indicated the narrow brown bottle of Old Fitzgerald he carried in his fist. "I always take some when my arthritis acts up. We'll give him enough so he's numbed up but good."

Zurina dragged her gaze off him. Leveled it over Trey.

"You will not touch him," she said slowly. Succinctly.

"He'll die if we don't get that bullet out."

"He needs a surgeon."

Not a cattleman who would just as soon see him dead than live to raise sheep.

"Yes," Trey said. "He does. But it's not possible, is it?"

"I will make it possible."

"How?" he demanded.

"I will find a way."

"You going to carry him on your back into town?"

"If I must."

He made a sound of impatience. "Like hell you will."

Zurina knew her words were only false bravado to him, but she meant each one. They made clear her intention to do everything she could to give Papa the help he needed.

And yet…

"When did he get shot?" Trey asked.

It was as if he knew the way of her thoughts. That too much time had passed already, and what had she done so far to help him?

Too little, too late?

"Last night," she said, miserable. "At supper."

He squinted an eye into the sky. "It's after dawn. The next day. What do you figure, Nub? Ten, twelve hours, maybe, he's been carrying that bullet?"

"Reckon so." The old cowboy rubbed his grizzled jaw. "Something's got to be done for him, ma'am. And pretty damn fast, I'd say."

As if tugged out of his faint by the sound of their voices, Papa moaned and stirred. Awash in sympathy for all he'd endured, and for what still lay ahead, Zurina touched his cheek tenderly, and felt the heat of his fever.

"Too bad the lady doesn't want our help." Sighing loudly, Trey stood. "Let's head out, Nub. We've got a helluva lot of riding ahead of us."

The cowboy pursed his lips, chapped from the wind and sun. "Yep, we sure do. Guess we could leave her a knife, couldn't we? Then she could build her own fire to get the blade good and hot. She'll just have to find a way to hold her daddy down by herself while she pushes that white-hot knife into his shoulder. 'Course, it won't be easy finding the lead in there. Might take her a while, but she'll figure it out."

With a careless shrug, Nubby pivoted on his boot heel and strolled over to Trey, already bending to grasp his horse's reins.

Zurina gritted her teeth. Hated herself for giving

in to their manipulation. And hoped Papa would forgive her.

She abruptly stood. "Wait!"

She held her breath, the fear racing through her that they wouldn't listen, after all. That they'd mount up and ride off like they said they'd do, and leave her alone.

To let her father die.

Her heart pounded as Trey Wells straightened, in no hurry, and locked his gaze with hers.

But he said nothing. Merely waited. Forcing her to make the next move.

The bastard.

Clinging to every shred of pride she had left, she lifted her chin.

"Please," she said.

"Please what?" he taunted in his low voice.

"Please do not go."

From somewhere deep within her core, the plea came. This need to trust in Trey Wells, just this once.

What choice did she have?

Perhaps it was only Papa's elevated opinion of him. Or perhaps it was that neither he nor Nubby were wearing bandannas and had not harmed her or her few remaining sheep when they'd had every chance to do so.

Whatever the reason, she couldn't deny she needed

Trey Wells. Needed him so much she was willing to get down on her knees and beg him to stay.

He dropped the reins and moved toward her in a slow, purposeful tread. A part of her, the female part, noted the grace with which he walked. The control he showed. The power he was accustomed to wielding. An awareness that flickered through her with a startling and unexpected clarity.

He came to a halt in front of her. His stance forced her to tilt her head back a bit to hold his hard gaze.

"Tell me your name," he said.

"Zurina."

It never occurred to her to withhold the information. She didn't expect him to know her. They'd never met, after all.

But clearly, he hadn't recognized her father. Most likely he would have, under different circumstances, when Papa would've spoken to him with his usual respect.

Circumstances when he wasn't laying unconscious on the ground, his pale cheeks covered in a short beard. Sick and wounded.

"Zurina," Trey said, as if testing the unusualness of her name on his tongue.

"Vasco," she finished. "Zurina Vasco. You already know Papa."

For a moment, he appeared stunned. "Gabirel?"

She nodded. "Yes."

His glance whipped downward with a muttered

oath, and he dropped into a squat beside her father again, gripped his chin and swiveled his head gently to study his features. As if to see for himself if Zurina spoke the truth.

"I'll be damned." His jaw hardened, when he realized she had.

"Is he the sheepman who grazes over in the valley?" Nub asked with a frown.

Trey nodded. "Yes. Sun River."

"Hell." Nubby thrust the flask of whiskey toward him. "Best get this over with."

Trey turned grim. He slipped his arm beneath Papa's shoulders and raised him to a half-sitting position. Papa groaned. Trey took the whiskey from Nubby and held the bottle to her father's lips.

"Drink up, Gabirel," he said. "You'll soon be glad you did."

And Zurina knew his ordeal was about to begin.

Trey wasn't sure who worried him more—Gabirel or his daughter.

Zurina.

Zurina Vasco.

He committed her name to memory while his gaze clung to her slender form, the concern building in him as she knelt at the riverbank, washing her face. Trying to regain the composure she'd lost.

Taking the bullet out had cost her. She'd felt her father's pain deeply, as if she'd experienced the knife on her own shoulder, and the anguish had been more than she could handle. She'd fled toward the river, only to lose the contents of her stomach before she got there.

But then, the smell of burning flesh would upend anyone's belly. At the time, Trey had wrangled with a healthy dose of revulsion from it himself.

The worst had been Zurina hearing her father's screams. Trey grimaced. Yeah, that'd been the worst. Nubby had done all he could do to hold the man down while Trey probed the muscle with the knife's blade, then doused the wound with a good amount of whiskey in hopes of staving off infection. After Trey finished the nasty job of cauterizing, Zurina had bolted and Gabirel had passed out.

Tiredly Trey lifted his Stetson and ran a hand through his hair. Main thing was, Gabirel had gotten through it, the damned bullet was out, and all that was left was getting him to a hospital.

The whole ordeal had set Trey back in his need to find Allethaire—and his father's murderer. But finding her had to come first. He'd accomplished nothing since he left the ranch last night, save for learning she hadn't returned to her hotel in Great Falls.

He could only hope she'd gone back there by now and was safe, sleeping off her aggravation with him. Or maybe sleeping satisfied that she'd given him a damned good scare.

It'd be just like her, he knew. Still, when it was

all said and done, she'd have her father to contend with. Paris would disapprove of her running off like she did. He wouldn't appreciate the scandal she'd caused, either. Wasn't proper for someone in their social status.

Like Sutton, Paris saw Allethaire's marriage to Trey as an extra-fine bonus for the hydro-electric plant he wanted to build on Wells rangeland, and Trey knew it well enough.

But Paris had to understand Trey's decision to postpone the engagement, which spurred Allethaire's decision to run off in a huff. Trey refused to tolerate her behavior, this time and any other time in the future. Like it or not, both had to accept his refusal to leave Montana.

Zurina straightened from the riverbank, and like a cloud of fickle butterflies, Trey's thoughts scattered away from Allethaire to gather over Zurina again. She appeared calmer, in control. She strode toward him with her back straight, her shoulders squared, and from the way she held her chin, her pride carried tight around her.

She was a beauty, all right, even dog-tired from all she'd been through. That dark skin, hair black as midnight—her Basque heritage shown strong in her coloring and gave her an exotic look different from other women he knew.

Different from Allethaire, he mused. About as different as two women could be.

Allethaire went to great lengths to keep the sun off her face, and Zurina, well, she seemed to welcome it. She didn't appear to notice how the wind had tossed her hair, that it all dangled loose and free down to her waist. Allethaire kept hers pinned up close around her head to keep a single strand from escaping. Hell, Trey had never seen it any other way.

Zurina drew closer, and he chastised himself for comparing the two women. Wasn't fair to either one of them, and their differences shouldn't matter, besides.

He rose slowly to meet Zurina, and their gazes met. She had a strange pull to those eyes of hers. They kept hold of his and wouldn't let go.

"What happens next?" she asked coolly.

"We get him to a hospital."

"Yes." A tinge of impatience colored the word. "But how? They took our horses."

Trey had noticed the team was gone. He'd hoped the horses had simply run off into the hills in last night's chaos and would've found their way back to water by now.

But no such luck. Whoever attacked the Vascos's camp had a price to pay. Trey wasn't going to tolerate the crime on his land, and he would see to it whoever was responsible would suffer the consequences.

He just had to get Gabirel to the hospital first.

Then, he had to find Allethaire—and his father's murderer, too.

Helluva a list, for sure.

"We'll make a travois. Nubby is out looking for some stout branches," he said. "Won't take long, and we'll be on our way."

Her lips thinned, and she gave him a curt nod, then knelt next to her father, still sleeping off the whiskey and the effects of Trey's surgery.

She caught the hem of her skirt, which dripped wet from a dunking in the river, and gently dabbed at his sweaty forehead, his flushed cheeks and along the curve of his neck.

Trey knew he should leave. Help Nubby find those branches. It'd cut the time in half if he would, but something compelled Trey to stay right where he was.

A reluctance.

He knelt, too, beside Gabirel and watched Zurina minister to him. His gaze followed her hand, noted the slenderness of her fingers, the short, clipped nails. The tender way she cared for him.

Was clear as red paint how much she loved her father, and words to assure her he'd likely be all right, that Trey intended to do what he could to help them both with the loss of their flock, hovered on his tongue.

But before he could say them, she speared him with a hard glance.

"I will never forgive you for this," she said.

Startled, he drew back. "What's that supposed to mean?"

Her glance dropped to her father again, her cooling strokes never faltering. "Exactly what I said."

"What?" he insisted. "Taking out the bullet? Making him hurt?"

"No." Her expression revealed she considered him an idiot. "This." Her arm swept outward, indicating the lifeless mounds scattered over the range. "What you have done."

His eyes narrowed while his brain wrestled with confusion. "What have I done?"

For a long moment, she didn't respond but kept her attention fixed on a lamb, roaming aimlessly over the grass. Looking lost. Bleating for his mother.

But no ewe responded. No mother went to him.

Zurina's eyes welled, and she smoothed back the hair from her father's forehead.

"Do you think I'm so stupid that I don't know, Mr. Wells?" she said.

To demand again that she explain herself would only make him appear like the idiot she already considered him to be. Trey held his tongue, but he leveled her with an unrelenting glare.

She emitted a sound of disgust, released her skirt hem and stood. She would've strode away from him if Trey hadn't stood, too, stepped around her father and grasped her elbow before she could.

His fingers firm, he turned her toward him. She

wriggled beneath his grip, and he almost lost his hold, but in a quick movement, he grasped both her shoulders and kept her firmly in front of him.

He scowled. The top of her dark head reached his chin. Beneath the soft cotton of her blouse, he could feel the warmth of her skin, the tension in her muscles. The strength in them, too, gained from her daily routine of work.

"I hate you," she spat.

"Sorry to hear that, Miss Vasco," he said, letting the sarcasm creep into his drawl. "But I guess I don't much care if I don't even know why you would."

That she showed no gratitude for what he'd done to save her father's life didn't surprise him much. Whatever stirred up her hate and got it to festering would've pushed gratitude to the bottom of her list.

"Does it make you proud to show kindness to the sheepman when you know deep in your heart you're a hypocrite?" she taunted.

He stared down at her. "A hypocrite?"

"And yet you send others to hurt him. The flock that he needs to survive."

"Me?"

"Yes, you. Trey Wells. Who is no more than a coward and a hypocrite!"

"Hell." He gave her shoulders a shake. Whatever the hell she was accusing him of made no sense. And made him just plain mad, besides.

"Listen here, woman. You're talking crazy. If you're saying I was responsible for what happened out here, you're wrong. Dead wrong. Y'hear me?"

Scorn darkened her expression. "You lie. I saw—"

"What?" he cut in sharply. "What did you see?"

Her chin jerked up. "Horses with the Wells Cattle Company brand."

Stunned, Trey released her. "What?"

"It's true."

"The men who did this to you, to your flock, rode WCC horses?"

"Yes."

"Impossible."

Or was it?

The entire outfit had attended his father's funeral yesterday. Every man, down to the youngest wrangler. Trey knew it for a fact, had seen them with his own eyes, both at the church and afterward at the ranch, at the luncheon.

Each man in his outfit had been on the WCC payroll for a good long while. Trey would've known if one of them hated sheep so much that he would have massacred the Vasco flock.

While the likelihood wasn't impossible, it was damned unlikely.

Wasn't it?

Chapter Five

For the tiniest of moments, she was tempted to believe him.

Zurina stopped herself in time.

Of course, Trey Wells would deny his involvement in the killing of her sheep. Wasn't that the coward's way? To send his men to do his dirty work and save himself from sullying his precious reputation?

But even as her mind accused him, her instincts puzzled over his reaction.

Impossible.

He spoke the word with conviction. With thinly veiled anger. As if he took grave offense that she thought him—or his men—capable of such a crime.

"I don't know what game you're playing with me, woman," he growled. "But I've got no patience with it."

"What'd she say, Trey?" Nubby paused in mid-stride with the two long branches he'd been dragging behind him. "That them sheep killers was riding WCC horses?"

He appeared so appalled, Zurina's hatred wavered again.

"That's right, Nub." Trey's features filled with disgust, and Zurina knew every bit was directed at her. "That's what she claims. Ever hear anything so far-fetched?"

"None of the boys would—"

"I know."

Trey pivoted on his boot heel, strode toward his horse and untied the wool blanket rolled tight behind the cantle.

"I saw their brands." Her mind replayed the horrors from the night before. "There were two men, both wearing bandannas. One rode an Appaloosa, the other a spotted gray. The man on the gray did the killing, and the other—"

Her fingers flew to her lips. And in that moment, like a slew of angry crows, doubt pecked at her convictions, tearing holes into her hate for Trey Wells. If he had indeed planned the massacre against Vasco sheep and sent his men in his place, why would they kidnap the woman he intended to marry?

Had she been wrong about him all along?

She fought a horrified sting of tears.

"The other what?" Trey demanded.

"He took her. Your betrothed. I am sorry." Regret spiraled through Zurina in leaps and bounds. "I am so sorry."

For a moment, neither man moved. Then, the blanket slipped from Trey's fingers and landed on the ground with a dull thud.

"Allethaire? She was here?" he thundered.

"Yes." Zurina's head bobbed.

Nubby dropped the branches, one after the other. He pointed toward the ground. "Here? As in *right* here?"

"Yes."

The men exchanged stunned glances. A muscle ticked in Trey's jaw, and he turned back toward Zurina. Took a slow purposeful step toward her. And then another.

He looked so furious, tendrils of fear sprouted inside her. He was a powerful man. Lean and strong and obviously capable of great violence. Did he intend to hurt her, like his masked cowboys had done last night?

She took a wary step backward and barely kept from tripping over her father, still sleeping on the ground behind her.

"Start from the beginning." Trey halted. "Tell us everything."

Nubby strode forward, too, and stood at his side. "When did you see her?"

"Last night. She was lost," Zurina said, gathering courage from the information she had—and they needed. "She couldn't find her way back to the main road."

"Into Great Falls?" Trey asked.

"Yes."

"How did she get off it?"

"I don't know."

"All she had to do was—"

"I don't know." Zurina refused to speculate. "But she'd been drinking."

"Drinking!" Nubby exclaimed.

Trey cocked his jaw. "How much?"

She hesitated. "Too much."

His darkening expression revealed he could hardly comprehend it. "Keep talking."

"She wanted my father to take her back to the road, but it was too far. And soon too dark," Zurina said.

"He refused?"

"Yes." She didn't care if Trey felt Gabirel Vasco should have done as his betrothed demanded. "Papa insisted she spend the night with us. I made her supper, but before we could eat, they came."

"The men who killed your sheep," Trey said.

"Yes."

"The ones who were riding WCC horses."

Did he believe her now? Or was that skepticism she heard in his tone?

"Yes," she said.

"And then what happened?"

"He shot Gorri and—"

Zurina's voice broke. After the massacre, after the cowboys had left, it'd been incredibly hard carrying the sheepdog's furry body away from the wagon, out of Papa's sight. And her own. Their grief had been strong, overwhelming. Somehow, it'd been easier to lay him with the sheep who had suffered the same fate. It was how Gorri would've wanted it—to be with the flock he loved so much.

"Who's Gorri?" Trey asked.

"Our dog."

He nodded once, grimly, but said nothing.

"After he shot Gorri, he shot Papa, then he set the wagon on fire." She trembled from the nightmare, the haunting terror that would never in a million years leave her. "Allethaire was inside, hiding—"

"Hiding?"

"They were your men."

"They were not my men."

"She thought you'd sent them to find her."

"And if I had?"

"She would have refused to go."

"The hell she would."

Clearly he considered the notion unbelievable.

But Zurina had no intention of debating the point with him. Whatever problems he had with the woman were his own.

"When he learned who she was, when he found

out she was your betrothed, he—he grabbed her," she said.

"God Almighty," Nubby breathed.

"Did he say why?" Trey demanded.

"He said—" she clawed through the horrific sequence of events in her mind "—that you would bargain for her."

"He's looking to line his pockets," Nubby muttered.

"Whoever 'he' is." Trey slashed his attention back to Zurina. "Was she all right? Did they hurt her in any way?"

An image of how the cowboy backhanded Allethaire surfaced. For Trey's sake, Zurina schooled her features. "She was as well as could be expected."

His mouth tightened, and Zurina knew he wasn't fooled.

"Where were they headed?" he growled.

"I don't know."

"You didn't see which direction?"

"No."

Miserable, Zurina admitted the truth. The nightmare—it wouldn't end. The merciless shooting of the sheep, the roar of the fiery flames, her father's cries, and oh, the terrible fear that the masked cowboys would kill them, too.

Zurina had been powerless to save Allethaire. The cowboy had ruthlessly ridden off with her into the darkness—and Zurina had been so afraid for Papa, for the sheep…for herself.

If only she could have helped Allethaire. Could have foreseen what the cowboys intended. Could have been quicker to react.

But she hadn't. She'd failed everyone, including her flock.

And now, she'd even failed Trey Wells. Despite her opinion of the man, and his of the sheepman, his concern for the woman he intended to marry ran deep. Zurina's heart hung heavy in her chest.

"Did you get a good look at either of them?" Trey demanded.

"No." She endured a new wave of regret.

"Nothing to remember them by? A scar? What they were wearing?"

"They were wearing bandannas. I noticed no more than that."

"Nothing to help us find them?"

He sounded so desperate, so keen on some detail that Zurina's sense of failure intensified.

"No." She swallowed. "I am sorry."

Again that muscle leaped in his cheek. His glance swung toward Nubby. "They could be anywhere."

Looking overwhelmed, the old cowboy blew out a breath. "Yeah."

"And they have half a day on us."

Zurina could almost forget the dislike she'd long

felt for Trey Wells as a cattleman, so great was her guilt.

"Let's get moving," he said.

Zurina's pulse jumped with sudden trepidation. What did they plan to do? Leave her? With Papa so sick? She had nothing with which to care for him, not anymore, and if they left her alone out here, he would surely die—

But at Trey's terse order, Nubby grabbed one of the branches he'd dropped. "Won't take long to rig the travois."

Trey retrieved the wool blanket and tossed it toward him, then untied his lariat from the saddle. "Hand me the ends, Nub. I'll lash them together."

Her stare fixed on the strange contraption they set out to build, and her instincts assured her they wouldn't take the time to do so if they didn't intend to use it for her father's benefit.

"I don't know what a travois is," she said carefully, unfamiliar with the word.

"It's the best we can do for a wagon," Trey said. He didn't bother looking at her while he settled the crisscrossed ends over Nubby's saddle horn and tugged them into place against the horse's neck. "We'll stretch a blanket over the branches to make a bed. Gabirel can rest on it while we ride into Great Falls."

The unlashed ends made a wide "V" and would drag on the ground during the ride. Perhaps it wouldn't jostle him unduly, but even so, it was better than nothing and would get them where they needed to go.

A hospital, as fast as they could.

"See what you can salvage from your wagon," Trey commanded. "We'll be heading out soon."

For a moment, incredible relief held Zurina rooted.

Until the realization slammed through her that she was beholden to Trey Wells for his help. That she was completely vulnerable and helpless without it, without him, and how could she do anything else but accept it?

Accept help from a cattleman.

Zurina swallowed her pride and hurried to comply, all the while very much aware that they only had two horses. If Papa rode on the travois hitched to Nubby's, Trey Wells intended to have her ride with him.

And her belly unexpectedly fluttered at the prospect.

"Is there anyone you should send word to?"

Trey's low voice swirled near her ear and raised gooseflesh on her skin. Zurina blamed her foolish reaction on her place in front of him. On his horse.

An intimate position, for sure, the way their bodies rocked together during the ride, their thighs pressed against the other's. Trey's hand gripped the reins near her hip.

Much too intimate.

The proximity of him so close behind her left her muscles stiff from tension. Made her ache to put distance between them, to give herself room to breathe. To relax.

But mostly, so she could think.

She didn't know what to do with her feet, since his claimed the stirrups, and her legs dangled and bumped into his again and again. Worse, fatigue had been unrelenting. Despite her haste to get her father to Great Falls, she had an almost overwhelming urge to lean backward into Trey Wells's chest, help herself to the solid warmth of his body and fall asleep.

Almost.

To do so would be the biggest mistake of her life. Leaning on him—literally or figuratively—would mean she trusted him.

She didn't.

She couldn't.

She would never forget he was Sutton Wells's son. A cattleman's son.

"Miss Vasco?"

He leaned inward, and the brim of his Stetson appeared in the tail of her eye. His chest pressed into her shoulder, and startled that he'd spoken, she jerked back, gripping the saddle horn to steady herself.

"Thought maybe you'd fallen asleep," he said.

"No." She refused to be so weak. Or allow him to think she was. "My mind was on other things, nothing more."

His inspecting gaze lingered, just long enough to flaunt the coppery glints in his eyes and reveal how they were ringed with coffee-brown. Lashed with thick crescents, too, and grooved by tiny lines at each corner. Lines etched from untold hours squinting in the sun.

That she could notice so much about him appalled her, and she angled her face away—to keep from looking at him at all.

He drew back. "I asked if there was someone you needed to send word to about what happened. Family or friends who'd want to know."

"Yes." Everyone she knew would be devastated. "My uncle, Benat, who is Papa's brother. And my cousin, Deunoro."

But of anyone, she yearned to tell Mikolas most. Except she had no idea where he was, where he'd been these past weeks, and she missed him, needed him, terribly. More than ever.

He would know what to do. He'd help her make the right decisions, find a way to pick up the pieces. To start over.

But mostly, he'd help her get even.

Now, Zurina had to do all those things herself, once Papa received the medical care he needed.

At the thought of him, she twisted and peered down the road. In the distance, Nubby followed at a slower, more careful pace with the travois attached to his horse,

Zurina had agreed with Trey's decision to ride into Great Falls ahead of them. By the time Nubby arrived with Papa, Zurina would have found a doctor to care for him. And Trey would have set into motion a plan to hunt down Allethaire.

Justice, at its fiercest.

Zurina sensed the fury he kept coiled tight inside him. She could almost taste the heat of it. Trey refused to tolerate the wrongs done to him and the woman he intended to marry, and Zurina knew it was only a matter of time before he settled the score.

She might have marveled at his control if she hadn't been all too aware that she was responsible for his troubles. If they hadn't left Sun Valley and ventured onto his range to graze their flock, then Allethaire Gibson would never have been kidnapped.

Kidnapped.

Oh God. The immensity rocked through her. Just thinking the word and all it implied unearthed ugly memories from a time deep in Zurina's past that she'd learned not to think about, but she thought of them now, in all their horror. Her heart curled with anguish for what the poor woman was going through. She knew how terrified Allethaire would be. How helpless. And anxious. How *desperate* for escape.

Zurina willed Allethaire strength. And hope. But mostly, she prayed for Allethaire to trust in those who loved her, especially the man who would do all he could to find her.

Trey Wells.

Zurina knew she and her father were a burden to him. A certain and frustrating delay in his need to find her. That he made the effort to see to their needs first when he easily could have abandoned them out on the range to see to his own, well, Zurina had to concede it was a streak of honor she never expected to see in him.

"Do they live nearby?" Trey asked. "Your uncle and cousin?"

A deep breath helped clear her head. She couldn't dwell on the past, nor could anything from last night be changed.

She must concentrate instead on the future, for she had a score to settle, too. Her own share of wrongs to right.

"Yes," she said, pointing into the distance. "Over there."

The city of Great Falls lay sprawled before them, but beyond its boundaries, into the hills, was a small settlement comprised of her people. The majority of them Basque sheepherders, like Papa.

Zurina had never lived anywhere else but in that little village. She was related in some way to almost everyone who lived there. If word of her flock's massacre hadn't reached her family and friends by now, it would soon, and they'd be terrified for her and Papa's welfare.

Outraged, more.

"I'll make sure they're notified," Trey said as they approached the main street in Great Falls. "They'll want to ride in and see you and Gabirel."

"Yes," she said. "Thank you."

Zurina spoke her gratitude, though she was perfectly capable of notifying her family herself. Yet the crisp, businesslike tone in Trey's voice kept her from telling him as much. Clearly he played out a strategy in his head. She would do well to listen.

"When we get into town, I'll take you to Dr. Shehan's office. He was my father's physician for years. He'll give Gabirel good care."

Zurina stiffened. Sutton Wells's physician?

"Afterward, I'll head over to see the police chief and report what happened, then I'll round up a posse." His fist clenched over the reins. "I've lost too much time already."

Knowing he had, that they both had, Zurina said nothing to his plan but instead murmured a guilt-ridden prayer that Allethaire was all right. If not altogether safe, at least free from harm and soon reunited with Trey Wells.

But more than that, Zurina prayed the men who attacked her and her father would one day soon burn in hell.

Chapter Six

Oblivious to the trouble in Trey's upended world, Great Falls bustled with its normal routine of activity. Rigs rumbled up and down the dirt streets. Boardwalks clattered from the footsteps of women and children hurrying through errands and appointments. Storekeepers propped open their doors to let in the day's freshness and beckon customers. Dogs barked. Horses whinnied. Men shouted.

Trey hardly noticed. He could only think of how he had to find Allethaire.

Fast.

He reined in at the front of Doc Shehan's medical office, dismounted and tied the leathers to the hitching post. By the time he turned back to help Zurina out of the saddle, she was already down on the ground.

Clearly she wasn't accustomed to a man's assistance.

Or maybe she had no desire to accept his.

Trey had few misconceptions about her resentment for him. From the moment she'd first aimed that rifle barrel at his chest, she'd made her dislike pretty damn clear.

Trey could understand her reasons. Seeing those brands on the horses last night, believing the men who killed her sheep worked for the Wells Cattle Company and were sent by him—yeah, he could understand her resentment.

But she had to understand he wasn't the lowlife she thought he was. Somehow, he had to find a way to prove to her the truth. Answers about who those men were, why they had WCC horses in the first place. Why they chose to attack the Vasco flock. Why they kidnapped Allethaire. And another wild thought to add to the bunch—if they had anything to do with his father's death.

Trey couldn't figure any of it, though he'd considered every angle, up one side and down the other. After his father's murder, to have this happen—did it all fit together? Or were they random incidents?

Trey itched for answers. For revenge. He intended to get both, not only for his own sake…but for Zurina Vasco's, too.

He stole a moment to study her while she stared down the road on which they'd ridden in, looking worried for Nubby and her father to appear. The scent of smoke and charred wood clung to her clothes, her skin, her hair. But somehow that smell suited her— like the outdoors. Natural and unpretentious.

Trey could see the weariness in her heavy-lidded gaze and the paleness of her cheeks, but her spirit still ran strong. Easy to see that, too. Not once had she complained. In spite of all she'd lost, the burden of despair that weighed on her shoulders, she carried her chin high, thinking more of her father than of herself.

Seeing it, knowing it, something moved in Trey's chest. He allowed himself to stop thinking of Allethaire—and to think of this Basque woman instead.

Gently he gripped her chin and turned her face toward him. "Zurina."

Her startled glance flew to him, but she didn't pull away.

"Do you mind if I call you by your first name?" he asked.

Her shoulder lifted in a tiny shrug. "It's what I am used to."

A difference between their people, he realized. His own preferring more formality in using the term 'Miss' when addressing someone they'd just met.

"Call me Trey," he said.

"Why?"

"Because I want you to trust me."

Her brow shot up. "Trust you?"

The way she said it, slathered with derision, left him with the distinct feeling he was wasting his breath.

But he kept going.

"I'm hoping your calling me by my first name will be the first step in doing that," he said.

Her gaze sharpened. "I don't think so. Not until I find the truth."

"You think I don't want to find it, too?" he demanded roughly.

"Trey! Trey Wells!"

At the woman's voice, Zurina stiffened and pulled her chin from his grasp. Hiding his frustration, vowing to find another opportunity to convince Zurina, he turned and spied Emma Hill, hurrying toward him on the boardwalk. Martha, her large-boned mother, lumbered beside her.

Trey hid a grimace. The women were the daughter and wife of James Hill, a railroad magnate with the Great Northern Railway. James, along with Paris Gibson, hoped to partner with Trey in building the hydro-electric plant. And Martha, well, she hoped to wrangle a marriage with Trey for Emma. The fact that he'd chosen Allethaire didn't seem to matter most days. Martha had more nerve than she could hang on a fence. And Emma was a bona fide flirt.

"Hello, Emma. Martha." He lifted his hat in curt greeting.

"Why, Trey, I never expected to see you here!" Slightly out of breath, Emma halted and peered up at him with sagely wide eyes and a practiced pout. "Is everything all right?"

Trey thought through a reply. He had no idea how much they knew—they couldn't have heard about Allethaire's kidnapping yet, could they?

Instinct told him no—after all, he'd only found out himself a short time ago. They were far too calm, besides, and he had precious little time for hysterics.

"Been better, I reckon." He forced a smile.

She reached out and boldly laid a gloved hand on his chest. "You two had another spat, didn't you? That's why she left yesterday without saying goodbye to anyone."

"Allethaire?"

He played dumb. The Hills had gone to the funeral for his father and afterward attended the luncheon at the ranch. Obviously Allethaire's absence hadn't gone unnoticed, and speculation about his going after her would have been rampant.

Inevitable there'd be gossip, he knew. Some claimed Trey's marriage to Allethaire was the best love-match in all of Montana, ensuring construction of the hydro-electric plant along the Missouri.

"Of course 'Allethaire,' silly." Emma laughed, a little too gaily. "Really, you have such patience with her, Trey. Let me guess. She still wants you to move with her to Minnesota, doesn't she?"

"Running off from the funeral luncheon like she did with your daddy just barely in his grave and his killing still a mystery." Martha sniffed. "Why, her behavior is scandalous, if you ask me, Trey."

Which he hadn't. Trey kept one eye on the door to Doc Shehan's office and held back the retort.

"She's acting only for herself, that girl. Why, can you think of anything more selfish than expecting you to go back east with her? When Montana needs that power plant? Of course, you have your ranch to run, too, and you're needing to find Sutton's murderer. But she doesn't care about any of that."

"I'm in a hurry." Trey took Zurina's elbow and pulled her forward, so that she stood next to him. "I have a couple of matters to attend to."

But Martha kept her matronly body rooted in front of him. She waggled a finger at him with a smile that didn't quite reach her eyes.

"You know Emma loves Montana, Trey. She'll live in no other place. Isn't that right, Emma?"

"Hush, Mother." Emma slid a vaguely accusing glance at Trey. "Trey has a—a lady-friend with him, and I'm sure she doesn't want to hear our business."

"What?" Startled, the woman's glance slashed toward Zurina.

Mother and daughter took a discreet step backward. Their unified glances dragged over Zurina, from the top of her dark head with hair blown around her shoulders, past her plain blue cotton dress stained with her father's blood, and down to her feet, encased in dusty sandals.

"Sheep." Lips pinched, Martha drew herself up. "That's what I smell, Emma. Sheep."

Zurina sucked in a breath, as if the woman had spat in her face.

Trey gritted his teeth. "Mind your mouth, Martha."

"No, it's more smoky, Mother. I'd noticed it, too."

"It's both," Zurina said and yanked her elbow from between Trey's fingers. She speared him with a scathing glance, clearly blaming him for the Hills women's irreverence. "Excuse me."

Zurina shouldered her way between them with some irreverence of her own, and the pair were quick to give her room, but there was something about the way she all but ran into Doc Shehan's office that had Trey's feet moving after her.

"She's Basque, isn't she, Trey?" Emma asked, looking utterly confused.

Trey tossed her a cold glance. "Yes. She is."

"But you're a cattleman!" Martha protested. "And she's—"

"That seems to be the problem, doesn't it?" Trey shot back, impatient with their narrow-mindedness.

There wasn't much he could do about the prejudices between them, but he had to try. He left the two women gaping after him, pushed the good doctor's door open and strode inside.

The small sitting area held no waiting patients, but an elderly woman sat at a desk. She glanced up expectantly. Trey latched the door closed and ignored her.

Zurina stood with her back toward him, furiously finger-combing the tangles from her hair. In clipped, agitated movements, she swept the entire mass over one shoulder and separated the long strands into equal parts, her fingers flying as they formed a fast braid, and if she heard him come in, she pretended she didn't.

He knew her mad attempt at grooming herself was stung feminine pride, stirred up by Emma and Martha Hill. After their behavior, Trey couldn't much blame her. The two women had no idea what Zurina had been through, why she looked—and smelled—as she did. Bad part was, he wasn't sure it'd matter if they *did* know.

Suddenly Zurina spun toward him.

"What do you want?" she snapped.

She was a firecracker ready to explode, and he wasn't quite sure he could keep from getting burned.

His mouth pursed. He shouldn't be here, trying to soothe her wounded feathers, but he was, and he couldn't much help it. Time was ticking. He had to find Allethaire, but he delayed, just a little longer…

Zurina held the end of her braid between her thumb and finger to keep it from loosening. The way she glowered at him all but chased away any explanation he could muster up about following her in, and his brain scrambled for something intelligent to say.

He cleared his throat. "Looks like you need something to hold your hair together."

He rooted in the hip pocket of his Levi's and pulled out a short length of pale yellow ribbon. Allethaire's, left behind after a recent visit to the ranch. He'd always intended to return it to her, but never managed to remember.

Zurina might appreciate that he hadn't, considering she had nothing of the sort with her. But by the scathing way she glared at the thing, Trey feared it'd disintegrate into ashes. Her pride again, warring with indecision on whether to accept it from him. Or not.

Making the decision for her, he reached out and wrapped the narrow strip around the braid's end himself, right above her fingers. Slowly, as if she determined he made no more threat than that, her hand lowered. He fashioned a respectable-looking knot and gave it a testing tug, then let the ribbon tails dangle.

"Thank you," she said stiffly.

"You're welcome."

He laid the secured plait gently against her shoulder and noted the contrast of yellow against the deep obsidian strands that even tightly braided felt like silk against his finger tips.

Suddenly his imagination formed a hauntingly vivid image of what her hair would feel like, smooth and shining and fully unrestrained, sliding through his fingers, past his wrist and over his arm—

An image he had no business having, and he abruptly drew back.

"Did you have a reason to follow me in here, Mr. Wells?" she asked, her tone cool. Blatantly challenging. "If not, I must make arrangements for my father."

"Trey," he growled. "Call me Trey."

Doc Shehan's secretary announced her approach with a brisk click of heels on the wooden floor.

"Is everything all right, Mr. Wells?" she asked.

He dragged his glance off Zurina. "I'm bringing someone in. Gunshot wound."

"Gabirel Vasco," Zurina said, twisting toward her in appeal. "My father."

"The bullet's out, but Doc needs to take a look at him. Give him something for pain," Trey added.

"Certainly," the woman said with a quick, compassionate nod. "But where is the patient?"

"I think they're here now," he said.

The clomp of horse hooves compelled Zurina to swivel toward the sound. Nubby appeared on the other side of the plate glass window, drew up and prepared to dismount.

By the time the cowboy's boot soles hit the ground, Zurina was outside, depriving Trey of the opportunity to apologize for Emma and Martha Hill's insults. To make promises he wasn't entirely sure he could keep. And to tell her he would do what he could to find the men who killed her sheep.

But he couldn't reveal the unexpected longing which found its way inside him, a slow-growing fever to see her again. A need he could only acknowledge was there, now that it was time for him to leave.

To find Allethaire. He had to track his father's murderer, too, which left no room for this foolish reluctance burrowing into his blood.

It shouldn't matter he'd likely not see Zurina again. He had no choice but to shift his attention to matters far more dire. He'd done all he could for her and Gabirel. Besides, she didn't care whether he stayed or went. She'd made that as plain as the horn on his saddle.

Knowing it, he shot the secretary a terse glance. "Send me the bill for Doc's services."

Then, before she could agree, he left.

Chapter Seven

Two Days Later

Trey had all but given up hope.

He squatted along the banks of the Missouri River and splashed his face with cold water. The crispness of the sensation helped ease his fatigue, drained away the dust and grime from the trail, cooled his sun-beaten skin—but did little to salve his worry.

They'd found no sign of Allethaire or the cowboys who had taken her. Not a single clue, though Trey and the posse had been relentless. Nothing to give them some direction, a hint of which piece of Montana they should target in their search.

At least, he hoped Allethaire was still in Montana—and she was still alive.

Regret settled over his shoulders like a heavy iron

yoke. If he hadn't argued with her yet again over leaving Montana, if he hadn't wanted to end their engagement, if she hadn't slipped away upset and wanting to return to her parents' home in Minnesota, then she'd be safe now.

She'd vanished into thin air, and that scared the hell out of him.

He said that you would bargain for her.

Zurina's words replayed in Trey's mind for the hundredth time, her recantation of the events leading up to Allethaire's kidnapping.

Trey would do everything he could to get her back. She had to know he would, but damned if he knew how when he had no idea where to go next. How could the kidnapper wrangle a deal when he kept himself hidden, like a snake under a rock?

George Huys squatted along the bank next to Trey. As police chief for the Great Falls Police Department, he headed up the posse of men who'd banded together to hunt her down. There wasn't a man Trey trusted more, and George's two decades as a lawman proved him a formidable ally.

He'd assigned his only two officers in the department to scour the city itself and to keep close watch on Allethaire's hotel. But so far, not a word from either of them.

Not a word from anyone.

"There has to be a reason why they took her," George said. "Something besides the obvious."

River water sluicing down his chin, Trey glanced over at him. "The obvious being money, you mean." Grimly, he resettled his Stetson on his head and rose. "That's a good reason right there."

The lawman rose, too, and brushed at the dust on his black suit sleeve, the garb he always wore while on duty. Nearby, three men, including Nubby, remained in their saddles, savoring a well-deserved smoke.

"Ransom." George shook his head in disgust. "It seems to be the fashionable thing for criminals these days."

Trey was inclined to agree. Now that his father was gone, the Wells Cattle Company was all his. Every dime. Which made him a rich man.

For whatever reason, money or otherwise, the kidnapper was using Allethaire to get back at him. Maybe Paris, too, a wealthy man in his own right.

Might be, too, the scheme was meant as a backlash to the hydro-electric plant. Someone who wanted to thwart its development and impede progress in this part of the country.

Who was that someone? A couple of cowboys who ruthlessly took matters into their own hands? Or were they working for someone else? Someone Trey knew? Someone Paris or Allethaire knew?

"She's still out there," George said, squinting into the horizon. "Somewhere close. The way I figure it, she's no good to them dead. If it's money they want, they'll have to keep her alive to get it."

The harsh truth gave Trey a degree of comfort. Of hope.

"You sure that Basque woman didn't say anything else?" the police chief asked. "Give you some other clue we could go on?"

Zurina. She'd been on Trey's mind, too. Sometimes, he couldn't shake the image of her. She'd just be there. In his thoughts. In his worries.

That fever again, in his blood.

Wasn't right that he'd be thinking of her as much as he was. Could be that she was just so different from Allethaire. From other women he knew. Those black eyes of hers. Smooth olive skin. That fiery spirit and damnable pride.

But she was vulnerable, too. Zurina and her father had been wronged, more than they deserved. They'd taken a big hit from losing their flock. Far as he knew, they were innocent of anything that could've provoked the attack.

Maybe that's why she was on his mind so much. He felt sorry for her, that's all.

Just sorry.

"I told you everything she told me, George," he said, squinting at the horizon, too. "It all happened pretty fast for her."

"Understandable."

They both knew Zurina was their only link to the

cowboys. Injured as he'd been, Gabirel couldn't offer much in the way of details. Trey kept hoping Zurina might recall something she'd forgotten, anything that could help in the search.

His hope was persistent. Unshakable. An itch that had to be scratched—only by seeing her again. He'd have to take George and the posse with him and pay her a call. Ask her more questions.

Except Trey had no idea where she lived, and how would he find out? How long would it take until he did?

"Trey, look."

His musings vanished at the urgency in Nubby's voice; his glance darted in the direction his friend indicated. At the small herd of cattle running over the distant range, toward tree-covered highlands.

In split-second speed, realization hit Trey that for the past two days, the posse had been riding on Wells land.

And these were Wells's cattle.

What the hell?

Whoever herded them out here had no right to do so. Trey knew it for a fact—he was boss for his own outfit. And by the way the herd ran, the way the cowboys yelled—

"Rustlers!" he shouted, spinning toward his mount and catapulting into the saddle.

"Hee-yah! Hee-yah!" Nubby spurred his horse into a run and took off after them.

Trey wasn't far behind, and his mood turned foul in a hurry. Whoever got the damned fool idea to steal his cattle would soon wish they hadn't, and wasn't it just plain handy that he had the Great Falls police chief with him?

But shortly into the pursuit, Trey could see the thieves had too much of an advantage. The cattle were too spread out to round up anytime soon.

Cursing the air blue, surrounded by the thunder of the posse's pounding hooves, Trey kept riding, closer to the hilly highlands. He'd pretty much lost hope of gathering his stock into a tidy herd, but by God, he intended to get a good look at the men responsible.

Through the roiling dust, he kept his eye on one in particular. The leader, evidenced by the command in his yells, the terse way he kept waving his arm.

Blond hair. Riding an Appaloosa. Levi's and bandanna. Just like thousands of other cowboys.

Nothing about him felt familiar.

Suddenly the rustler's horse veered into a sharp right turn and disappeared into the woodlands. His accomplice escaped with the herd to the left, into the thick-growing pines. In moments, the entire bunch was gone.

Trey pulled on the reins to slow his mount. Fury sparked inside him, lighting a powder keg of frustration. Now he'd have to send Nubby back to the ranch, gather up the outfit and scour the hills to round the strays up again—while Trey continued searching for Allethaire.

Damn it, Dad. I wish you were here to help me.

It felt more surreal than ever knowing his father would never be able to. That he was forever gone, and Trey would never again lay eyes on his face, hear his deep laugh or his notorious string of hearty cussing when it was warranted. Or when it wasn't. Trey hadn't had a chance to tell him goodbye, or how much he loved him. They'd both been denied the luxury of making the most of the time they had left together.

I need you.

The loss tumbled through Trey in a sudden surge of tightly held grief. The burden of his responsibilities hung heavy on his shoulders, in his mind. These troubles he faced, the questions which demanded answers—finding Allethaire, his father's killer, avenging Zurina for the loss of her sheep, and now, the gang who rustled his cattle—Trey wasn't sure he could do it all.

The fear, the frustration, rolled through him. He could likely fail, and what then?

Why did you have to die? I need you, and it's not fair.

Sutton Wells possessed a strength and sense of righteousness that propelled him into the powerful man he was—before his life had been unfairly taken from him.

He'd know what to do.

He'd find answers—and a way to even the score. *It's not fair. Not fair, not fair.*

He'd expect Trey to do the same, in his place. The Wells Cattle Company and all the ideals his father once stood for, demanded it.

The knowledge infused Trey with renewed resolve, helped push back the wave of sorrow and hold it in submission. He couldn't allow himself to wallow in the anguish and unfairness of Sutton Wells's death.

The words to order Nubby back to the ranch hovered on his tongue.

Movement in the trees kept them there.

On either side of him, Nubby and George stiffened, telling Trey they'd seen the movement, too. All three of them reached for the revolvers strapped to their hips.

Trey stared hard at the small figure headed right toward them—at a full run.

"I'll be damned," George breathed.

"He's just a kid." Nubby sounded stunned.

Trey sheathed his weapon. Dismounted. He stepped around his chestnut sorrel and waited for the young boy to draw closer.

"Might be a trap," George warned under his breath.

Trey didn't see how a kid could much hurt them, but he braced himself for the unexpected. He figured the boy was barely ten, maybe older since he looked so small. Skinny and olive-skinned. As he ran closer, an oversize beret flopped on top of his shaggy-haired head.

Trey squatted on his haunches to meet him. Out of breath, with a grin as amiable as could be, the boy halted in front of him.

"Howdy," Trey said, making sure he grinned back. Whatever the child's purpose was in coming out of the highlands, Trey wanted him to know he had nothing to fear from any of them.

The boy righted his beret and peered up at the mounted men staring down at him. Wide black eyes revealed his curiosity. He showed no apprehension from being the object of the posse's sharp attention.

"My name is Trey Wells," Trey said and extended his hand for shaking. "What's yours?"

"Trey?" the boy repeated, his stare swinging back.

"That's right."

The youngster wore threadbare britches and a faded cotton shirt that had seen cleaner days. Only a few buttons held the thing on his scrawny shoulders. Trey held little doubt the kid lived in the hills, and most folks who lived up there were sheepherders.

Basque sheepherders.

"What's your name, son?" Trey asked again, firmer this time.

The youngster glanced down at the hand Trey kept extended toward him, but instead of returning the gesture, he planted a small piece of folded paper in Trey's palm.

Trey glanced down at the paper, up at the boy, then down again at the paper.

"This for me?" he asked in surprise.

But even as he voiced the question, he read his name on the outside in crude, bold lettering.

The youngster made some response in a language Trey didn't recognize. He appeared as genial as ever, in no hurry to leave.

So Trey unfolded the note and read its message:

> *$5,000 or your woman dies.*
> *Wolf Creek. Dusk. Tomorrow.*

Allethaire was still alive. He thanked God for it, but his blood ran cold at the message's sinister tone, and it was the two names at the bottom that had Trey staring the hardest.

Mikolas Vasco and Woodrow Baldwin.

"What's it say, Trey?" George demanded.

Troubled, Trey straightened and handed it to the lawman, who read the message, then handed it to Nubby. Who did the same and handed the paper back to Trey. Who read it all over again.

"Any of these names familiar?" he demanded.

"Woodrow Baldwin is." George shook his head

in disgust. "Has a small place down in Broadwater County. Runs a few cows, a few horses. Mostly rustled stock, from what I hear. Been charged with harassing sheepherders, too. That boy has been a burr under the saddle for the Broadwater sheriff for a while now."

"Sounds like he's moved on to bigger things," Trey said grimly.

"He's got to be stopped," Nubby said with a rare vehemence that caught Trey's attention.

"That's why we're out here, Nub," he said.

"Reckon this Mikolas Vasco is any relation to Zurina?" Nubby asked. "Same last name."

"She had nothing to do with the kidnapping." Instinct told Trey she hadn't. She'd been too distraught during the telling of the story. Too worried.

"You don't know her." The lawman spoke up. "She could be capable of most anything, and you wouldn't know it."

"Call it a gut feeling, George. Zurina had *nothing* to do with this."

"Zurina?"

Trey's head swiveled to the young boy, whose black eyes had lit up.

Trey squatted again. "Yes. Zurina. You know her?"

"Zurina." The boy grinned.

Seemed the boy didn't know English, but Zurina was one word he knew, and Trey had no intention of letting him go without wrangling a little help from him first.

Reaching into his hip pocket, Trey withdrew a pair of shiny silver dollars. He held them in his palm, and the black eyes fastened over them. Like a winter-starved wolf over a bone.

Trey had his attention all right. The nice thing about money? Everyone wanted some. Didn't matter how old they were. Or how young.

"Zurina." Trey took one of the coins and lazily turned it this way and that, letting him get a good look at it.

The kid nodded. Miraculously he turned and pointed toward the hills. "Zurina."

Relief poured through Trey from his victory. She lived up there, and the boy knew where. Trey dropped the coin into the grimy palm, and the boy's grin widened. His fingers closed, fast as a bear trap.

But Trey had one more coin left, and this time, the boy would have to work a little harder to earn it.

"Zurina," he said. "Take me to her."

The boy reached for the money, but swifter, Trey pulled his arm back.

"Take me to her," he said again and slowly, making sure the boy watched, he returned the coin to his pocket as an unspoken promise the money would wait until the job was done.

He rose, tucking the ransom note into another pocket for safekeeping.

The boy turned toward the highlands and began to walk, pausing once to glance over his shoulder, as if to make sure Trey followed.

"I'm going with him, George." Trey took the reins to his horse, but he didn't mount up. "Nub, head on back to the ranch. You know what to do to get our stock back."

The cowboy frowned. "But—"

"Go on. George, find a place where you can stay out of sight with the others. If you don't see me before, we'll meet up at Wolf Creek. Like the note said."

"You're not paying the five grand, are you?" the police chief demanded.

"Not one red cent, if I can help it," Nubby said, again vehement.

"If I can beat them at their own game, I won't have to pay them a thing," Trey said, grim.

"I'm telling you, you can't go up there alone," George commanded. "No telling what those folks will do to you."

If Zurina's people, led by her brother, banded together to bilk Trey out of thousands of dollars to ransom Allethaire, then Trey had no qualms.

"They've got what I need, and I've got what they want," he said. "I'll be fine."

Riding into the highlands with the posse in tow would scare the Basques, for sure. Better that they see the lawmen ride off. They wouldn't know the posse's intent to lie in wait. The ransom note gave Trey some time, enough to get Zurina to trust him. To do so, he had to let her know he meant her—and her people—no harm by entering her village alone.

Hoping his logic was sound, he grasped the reins firmly in his hand and followed the young Basque boy higher into the hills.

Chapter Eight

"Where the hell is he going?" Woodrow muttered to himself.

From his place deep amongst the pines, he watched them pass by. Why Trey was heading up the hill with that kid instead of riding away with the posse, Woodrow couldn't fathom.

But he didn't like it.

He strained to see the pair better through the latticework of needles and branches and pondered why the ransom note hadn't fazed Trey. Why didn't he act more worried about that whiny bitch he intended to marry?

Trey should've been hightailing it back to his banker and withdrawing that pile of money from fat WCC accounts instead of moseying up the hill, like he didn't have a care in the world.

Woodrow couldn't figure it, but he needed that money—and fast. He was going to hire a smooth-talking lawyer, and he was going to hire the best. One smart enough to knock Trey off his high horse and split that WCC empire into three equal parts.

Woodrow wasn't kin to having to take a smaller share than he'd first planned for, but with Mikolas added into the mix, it couldn't be helped. Now that Sutton was dead, the flow of bribe money had come to a screeching halt, and Woodrow's pockets were as dry as a tobacco box.

He wasn't proud he'd gotten so dependent on that bribe money, but he had. Sutton had paid top dollar to keep Woodrow out of his life and Trey's.

Up to now, Woodrow hadn't minded much. He'd bought his own spread down south a spell and tried to make it as a cattleman, just like dear ol' Sutton. But a few scrapes with the law had set Woodrow behind. Besides, why should *he* work hard when Trey had it so easy?

All that was going to change.

The old man had to be killed, or he would've killed Woodrow first. Woodrow had simply pulled the trigger in self-defense.

That's all it was.

Self-defense.

He held no regrets from the man's murder. After all, he'd never been given the chance to love Sutton Wells as he should. The way a son loves a father.

Only Trey Wells had been given the privilege. He alone had the love.

Not anymore.

Far as he knew, Woodrow and Mikolas were the only family Trey had left. With Sutton gone, the holdings of the Wells Cattle Company fell to Trey. All that land, those horses and cattle, money, power...

Wasn't fair one man should have so much.

Trey Wells would learn he had to share—with his two brand-new brothers. He'd soon see that Woodrow's rustling of the small herd of cattle was only the first step.

Allethaire Gibson was the second.

Thinking of her, a sudden urgency gripped him, and he mounted the Appaloosa, a gift he'd given to himself, compliments of the Wells Cattle Company. He was plumb out of patience with her sniveling and complaining, and he'd come close to backhanding her more times than he could count. But he'd always managed to restrain himself. It wouldn't do to hand his illustrious brother damaged goods, would it?

He'd left her behind under Mikolas's guard. Woodrow trusted the man well enough, but he was just so damned sullen, Woodrow couldn't figure what he was thinking most times.

Woodrow didn't like not knowing.

He shot a cautious glance downward, into the valley, and recalled how the posse's chase had been a call too close to repeat. He couldn't see any sign of them, though. Again, the lawmen's parting ways with Trey struck him as strange.

"Hoo hoodoo hooo hoo."

Woodrow's ears pricked at the sound. The call of an owl. Reggie had taught Woodrow all he knew about rustling stock, and he had a way with imitating birds, too. The great horned owl was his best.

Owls didn't call during the day, which meant this one signaled all was clear. Woodrow was only too glad to leave. He didn't yet know what Trey Wells was capable of. How far he would go to get back the woman he planned to make his wife. And what he was doing up there in those damn hills.

Whatever he intended, Woodrow had to be ready.

Cautious, he slipped out of the woodlands, into the open range and rode hard back to his hideout.

"What they do to you, Gabirel, we cannot stand for." Benat Ibarran slammed the tabletop with his meaty fist, his fury fairly spewing from his ears, like steam from a teakettle's spout. "The sheep are not like cockroaches, to be killed because Trey Wells does not want them on his land."

"If we do not stop the cattleman from destroying our flocks, we cannot live. We cannot survive." Deunoro Ugarti, Zurina's oldest cousin, fumed. "We will help you fight back, Gabirel."

She avoided looking at both men and filled her

father's glass with wine. In spite of all that had happened to the Vasco sheep, this talk of reprisal frightened her. How could the Basques retaliate against the cattleman when they were like little cubs against the mighty lion?

Never had she felt more hopelessness and a wavering of her resolve to fight back than now, after she'd experienced such terrible violence, such terrible *helplessness*, at the hands of the masked cowboys.

She blamed her dour mood on the downward turn her life had taken. How the reality of what they'd lost had set in hard.

She would never get the house Papa promised her. Never, ever. It would take years to build up the flocks again. Her life would be the same as it's always been—poor and struggling and boring. She would forever live in this tiny village as a sheepherder's daughter, without her mother to keep her company, without a husband to fill her nights, or children to fill her days…

The future had never seemed so bleak.

She blamed her mood on Trey Wells.

She couldn't shake him from her mind. He brewed in her a mass of confusion that twisted and snarled its way into every conviction she'd ever had about him.

"I don't believe Trey Wells is responsible for the killings, Uncle Benat," she admitted. "Not like I did at first."

"What?" Barrel-chested and double-chinned, he swung his black eyes toward her, and his voice boomed with demand.

Zurina reached across the table and refilled his glass, too. "He denies knowing of what happened."

She recalled how the grim set to Trey's mouth and the troubled shadows in his features seemed to prove it. He'd been clearly stunned from the destruction he discovered on his range.

If you're saying I was responsible for what happened out here, you're wrong.

"Pah! Of course he denies it." Uncle Benat's fleshy jowls quivered with outrage. "Is it not like a cattleman to lie and deceive whenever he can?"

You're wrong, you're wrong, you're wrong.

Trey's denial rippled through Zurina's brain, like a river slapping against its banks.

"His intended was kidnapped, Benat." With his good arm, Papa reached for his wine. "I saw it for myself. How do you explain that?"

Her uncle grunted and threw back a good-size swallow of his drink, as if he needed the time to think of a response.

Zurina poured the last of the wine into Deunoro's glass.

"It is merely a ruse," he said.

"How so?" Papa asked.

"He uses her and his men to cover the crime he commits, that is all."

Uncle Benat nodded and wiped his lips. "Clever, eh?"

Zurina refrained from rolling her eyes and stepped away from the table. She discarded the empty bottle, then took a plate heaped with slices of sourdough bread with one hand, a bowl of sheep's milk cheese with the other, and set both on the table.

"You are wrong about him," she said firmly, turning away to retrieve a new bottle of wine. "The accusations you make are ridiculous, even for a cattleman."

A moment of silence passed. She could feel three sets of dark-eyed stares on her back while she worked at tugging the cork free.

"You defend him, yet it is his brand you see on the horses they ride," Uncle Benat accused. "You tell us this yourself."

"Yes."

Zurina knew what she saw, but she didn't understand it. There had to be a reason why the WCC cowboys acted the way they did, without Trey's knowledge. A foolish risk, at best, and why would they bring such shame against him? The man who paid their wages?

Unless they weren't WCC cowboys at all.

Her glance met her father's, and she read the same questions, the same assumptions, in his gaze.

Though his skin remained pale, his lids droopy, he appeared a little stronger today, finding the stamina to slip from his bed to sit at the table for Uncle Benat and Deunoro's visit.

She had Trey Wells to thank for it.

Papa's life.

The care he received from Dr. Shehan, too.

Trey wouldn't have gone to such lengths to help Gabirel Vasco if he was behind the scheme to massacre the flock. But despite the help he'd given, there was nothing Trey could do to bring back the scores of sheep Papa had lost. Or revive Zurina's shattered dreams.

No one could.

Zurina knew Trey would be troubled about the identities of the men who had ridden WCC horses. And why. Of course, he would.

Falling pensive, feeling hopeless again, she set the open wine bottle in the center of the table and left Uncle Benat and Deunoro to their bluster.

She meandered over to the window, leaned a shoulder against the rough-hewn wall and peered through the dusty glass. Cabins as small and lackluster as her own dotted the hills. Basques who could no more afford a real house than she could. Friends and family who were destined to eke out a living under conditions rarely easy.

She knew everyone who lived in those ramshackle structures. And they knew her. They'd grieved over her mother's passing, expressed shock and dismay over Mikolas's absence and had been horrified at the news about what happened to Papa.

Those that raised sheep knew the massacre could've happened to their own flock, if fate had stepped in and deemed it so, and they'd been quick to show their worry, their concern, their compassion.

She would've done the same, and everyone meant well. But Uncle Benat and Deunoro could no more avenge the flock than they could fly to the moon.

Because they were sheepherders, unaccustomed to fighting. Her people knew only peace, hard work and survival.

Besides, who would they fight? Who were the masked cowboys? Where were they now?

Zurina couldn't consider Trey guilty of wrong-doing. Not anymore, and neither could her father.

She must cast Trey from her mind. With Mama and Mikolas gone, she must put aside her silly dreams of a real house. She must forget about revenge and concentrate on taking care of Papa. Together, some-how, they would find a way to make a new life.

Getting even with the masked cowboys would have to wait, but she would find a way, if it was the last thing she ever did.

The avowal trailed at the sight of a young boy traipsing up the narrow road. Her distracted glance fastened over him, and she recognized him as Ander Ibarran, her seven-year-old godson. Uncle Benat's youngest boy.

But who was that with him?

She stared harder. They drew closer. The man led a horse, a rich-coated chestnut, vaguely familiar. He wore his Stetson low over his forehead, shading his face, but that chiseled jawline, the broad build to his shoulders, the confident way he walked, almost a swagger—

A startled squeak escaped her lips, and she pressed her fingers to her mouth in a belated attempt to hold her surprise in.

Oh God. It couldn't be him.

He couldn't be here!

Her glance flew over her shoulder to the table, but neither Papa nor her uncle and cousin paid her any mind. Their wine and conversation absorbed them, their foolish talk of fighting the powerful cattleman, of taking on a man like Trey Wells—

And now he was here.

Just outside.

Getting closer with every pounding beat of her heart.

She feared what would happen if they saw him, what damage their old rifles would do. They wouldn't believe they'd be no match for him, that his power, his influence, would always outmatch theirs. Lowly sheepherders.

She inched backward to the door and hoped they wouldn't notice, then carefully pulled it open and slipped through to the outside. Latching the door again as quietly as she could, she pivoted, lifted her skirt and sprinted toward the man and boy coming up the dirt road toward her.

Oblivious to just who it was he had in tow, her godson heartily sang his favorite song, "Pintxo is our Dog."

"*...It's black and white, and it doesn't bite—*"

"Ander!"

Seeing her, both his stride and his song stopped. Zurina grabbed his hand and spoke in Euskara, the language of her people.

"Shh, sweetheart," she said, turning him. She would've felt guilty for hushing his boyish voice if she didn't have a dire need to keep his father and the other relatives from hearing. "Come this way."

"What's the matter, Zurina?" he asked.

She stepped toward Trey and grasped his hand, too, a part of her being jolted by the contrast of the two she held—one childish, the other very much male.

"Is there a problem?" Trey asked in his low voice.

Strong fingers closed around hers, a pleasant sensation if she would've allowed herself to dwell on it.

"There will be if anyone sees you," she said in a firm whisper.

She pulled them at a half-run toward a tangled thicket of cottonwoods growing not far off the road.

No one would glimpse them here—at least not without trying hard to—and once safely ensconced in the shadows, she released both their hands and turned toward Trey.

"What are you doing here?" she demanded.

"I need to talk to you."

About what, she couldn't imagine, but she hid her alarm. Did he intend to harass her *now* about how they'd moved onto his range from Sun River Valley? Or did this have something else to do with her sheep?

Whatever his need for her, she sensed its seriousness. She could see it etched in the darkened planes of his face.

Trey reached into his pocket and withdrew a folded piece of paper.

"Read this," he said.

She took the note and scanned the scrawled contents. Her apprehension burst into full-blown horror, and she forced herself to read the awful message again. Just to make sure she understood.

She understood everything. Including her brother's name at the bottom.

It couldn't be possible. Mikolas had nothing to do with Allethaire's kidnapping. He would never do anything so cruel, not to her, to Zurina, or to their papa's sheep the night Allethaire was kidnapped.

But the ransom scheme—had he fallen so low with

this—she read the name again and committed it to memory—this Woodrow Baldwin?

Evidently so. She recognized her brother's signature—he'd made that little curl at the end of the letter "M" for as long as she could remember.

"Where did you get this?" she asked hoarsely.

"From him." Trey gestured to Ander, watching them with wide eyes. "He was their messenger."

"What?" Little Ander? An innocent little boy? "How could that be?"

Trey's mouth twisted. "I have no idea. I was hoping you'd help me find out. We had a hard time understanding each other."

Zurina clucked her tongue. She'd forgotten the differences in their languages. "Of course. Uncle Benat speaks little English in his home."

"Who?"

"Ander's father. Benat believes it's important for his children to learn Euskara first. Then, when they are ready, they learn the English. I will do what I can to get the information we need from him."

Whatever part Mikolas played in the scheme, he had to be stopped. He was wrong in committing this crime, and so was Woodrow Baldwin.

Her brother's actions had to do with Sutton Wells and the terrible act he'd committed against their mother all those years ago. Zurina was all but sure of it. To Mikolas, everything was too fresh, too raw. As if their mother's rape happened only yesterday.

Clearly he was striking back at Trey, with Woodrow Baldwin's help.

She knelt in front of Ander, took his slender hand and kissed his knuckles affectionately. She wanted him to know he'd done nothing wrong, but the information she needed was very, very important.

Trey squatted next to her. "Start with asking him how he got the message. Who gave it to him?"

Zurina smiled at the young boy. She switched to speaking Euskara.

"Ander, sweetheart. We're going to ask you some questions. It's very important that you remember everything you can and tell me the truth. Do you understand?"

"Yes." His black-eyes bounced between her and Trey in curiosity. He nodded his head vigorously. His beret slipped, and he righted it again.

Zurina held the note in front of him. "Where did you get this?"

"A man on a horse gave it to me."

"Hmm." A broad answer, certainly. "Can you tell me what he looked like?"

"He had yellow hair." Ander's hand lifted to his neck. "Long to here. And he rode an Appaloosa."

She repeated the information to Trey. He nodded.

"I saw him. Have the boy tell his story from the beginning," Trey said.

At Zurina's urging, Ander launched into his tale.

"I was fishing in the stream behind our cabin, and the man with the yellow hair rode up to me. He was in a hurry and said there were some men in the valley. He said if I'd run real fast and gave Trey Wells his note, he'd give me these." Ander dug in his pocket and withdrew two pennies. He grinned. "See?" He peeped at Trey beneath his dark lashes. "And *he* gave me this." He added a silver dollar to the coins in his small palm. "I'm rich, Zurina!"

"Hmm. It seems you are."

She wasn't sure she approved of the bribery the two men used, but there was no help for it, she supposed. She relayed his explanation to Trey.

"He has this coming, too." Shifting, Trey fished in his hip pocket and added a second dollar to the pile Ander held. "I promised him the money if he'd take me to you. Let him know my thanks."

Zurina obeyed, and Ander beamed.

"Is there anything else you can tell us, Ander?" she asked. "Something you might've forgotten? Think real hard."

He shook his head and the beret dipped again. "I didn't forget anything."

Zurina fought disappointment. She hoped the man with the yellow hair, Woodrow Baldwin, would have mentioned Mikolas. Where he was. If he was safe. More important, if they were together, and where they both were hiding out.

But of course, that would be too easy. And Woodrow was too smart, too ruthless, to be so careless.

"Thank you, sweetheart." She enveloped Ander in a quick hug and rose. "You've been a good boy. A very big help to everyone."

"I have?"

"You have."

"Zurina? Know what?"

"What?"

Ander took her hand and pulled her back down to his level. Leaning close to her ear, he cupped his hand around his mouth.

"I think he likes you."

"What?" Startled, she drew back. "Who?"

Ander pulled her back again. "Trey Wells. He keeps looking at you. I think you should marry him."

"Ander Ibarran, that's the most ridiculous thing I've ever heard." Flustered, she straightened again and thanked the saints Trey didn't speak Euskara. "He's already intended for another."

The boy's expression turned intense, as if it suddenly became very important to coax her around to his way of thinking. "But he's rich and would make a good husband for you."

"I don't need a husband." His observation nipped her pride. Did she appear so pathetic, so unwanted, to everyone in her family? Even the children? "Besides, he's a cattleman. He would never marry me."

"But—"

"Even if I wanted him to. Which I don't," she added quickly. Firmly. "Now go. Do you still have some fishing left to do?"

He shrugged. "I guess."

"Then off with you." She swatted him on the backside and sent him scurrying out of the thicket, his coins clutched tightly in his hand.

"What secrets was he sharing with you?" Trey asked, eyeing her.

"He's merely worried about me, that's all." Zurina fastened her gaze on her godson, running up the road toward her cabin.

"Because of Woodrow? Or Mikolas?"

"Because of you."

It wasn't entirely the truth, she knew, and she turned back toward Trey, who had risen, too. Within the shadowed thicket, he stood tall, unexpectedly close. Crowding her. Making her aware of him in ways she shouldn't.

Like the way he smelled. Warm and male. Wind and saddle leather. He made her realize, too, how intimate, so very private it felt with just the two of them hidden in the trees.

She took a step back.

"You have no reason to be afraid of me," he growled with unexpected roughness. "What Woodrow did to you has nothing to do with me."

She knew it didn't, not like she once did.

"Well." She tossed her head. "What does Ander know? He's just a little boy, and all we learned from him was that the man who gave him the note was very likely Woodrow Baldwin."

"Did the man who took Allethaire have yellow hair?"

The vision of the cowboy assailed her memory. There'd been so much chaos. So much fear. But never would she forget what he looked like.

"Yes," she said.

"At least we have a name, then." Trey's jaw hardened. "That's something."

"Yes." Falling somber, she crossed her arms.

"Is Mikolas Vasco your brother, Zurina?"

She stilled at the low, cold timbre of his tone. This, then, was the true purpose in his coming. To hunt Mikolas down. To exact justice for Allethaire's kidnapping and what seemed to be his partnership with Woodrow for the crime.

She braced herself. "Yes, but—"

"Where is he?"

"I don't know," she said.

"He doesn't live up here with you? Or herd sheep somewhere close?"

"No. Not anymore."

The harsh glint in the coppery depths of Trey's eyes revealed his skepticism.

"Whatever you're thinking about him, you're wrong," she added.

"Am I?"

"He wouldn't hurt anyone, most especially a woman." *Not like your father hurt my mother.* Her mind screamed the words, but she bit them back. It was more imperative to convince Trey of Mikolas's innocence, or at least her conviction of it. "He wouldn't kidnap anyone, either. Not ever." Mikolas knew about kidnapping, what it was like. The horrors of such an ordeal, and—

"No way for you to know that for sure, Zurina."

"Of course, I know it for sure! He's my brother."

"How long has it been since you've seen him?"

Her lips clamped tight. She refused to reveal how many weeks it'd been. He'd only find fault with whatever she told him.

Trey grunted knowingly. "Long enough for him to steal WCC cattle or conspire with Woodrow for ransom?"

The words cut through her. It was all she could do to stand here and listen. To breathe through the pain.

"He would never do those things," she gritted.

"Five thousand dollars is a helluva lot of money, sweetheart," he drawled. "Men have betrayed for much less."

"Mikolas wouldn't betray anyone." Her hands curled into fists. How could she convince Trey? A man who despised sheepherders? "Are you going to tell me he wanted our flock killed, too?"

A moment passed.

"It doesn't make sense to me, either, Zurina," he said roughly.

"Because it couldn't possibly be true."

His grim silence revealed he didn't quite believe her. He would think she was covering her brother's whereabouts. Protecting him. And maybe...maybe she could understand him thinking that way.

"Everything I tell you, Trey, is the truth. This I promise to you." She paused and dared to open her heart to him. "It's very painful for my father and me not knowing where he is. What he's doing."

He appeared to digest her admission. And war with it. "I'll find him, Zurina. And when I do, if he's guilty, I'll even the score with him. Woodrow, too. They'll both pay for everything they've done." He paused, as if to drive his point home. "Everything."

"My brother wouldn't hurt anyone. He has honor. Principles. He wouldn't want to bring shame to his family and the Basque people."

"He already has. Can't you see? Unless—"

"Zurina!"

At the sound of Uncle Benat's booming voice, she whirled with a gasp. Trey's glance jerked over her shoulder.

Sure enough, there her uncle was. Standing on the edge of the thicket with Papa and Deunoro, all three of them holding their old rifles.

And each one was pointed at Trey.

Chapter Nine

Trey never heard the three Basques approach. He should have.

Now what was he going to do?

He wasn't much worried about the artillery they pointed his way. They had no reason to shoot him, at least not yet. It was Zurina who concerned him.

She appeared aghast at their animosity. As if their less-than-friendly behavior embarrassed her.

Trey couldn't much blame her. He wasn't kin to their behavior, either, but he might as well make the best of it.

"Mornin', gentlemen," he said. Or was it afternoon? He'd lost track. "No need for those shootin' irons, is there?"

"Ander tells us Trey Wells is here. A cattleman." A short, squat man with a protruding belly that strained his shirt buttons glowered. With that fur above his lip, he looked as fierce as a bitten boar. "He comes up here. He talks to Zurina, the boy says. After what happened to her, to Gabirel, we will fight to keep her safe."

Zurina emitted a sound of dismay and angled her body in front of Trey, as if to shield him from harm. "I am safe with him, Uncle Benat. Please put your rifle down."

Trey stepped forward, too, and smoothly nudged her aside. He took the privilege of reaching behind her and clasping her hip to keep her from moving in front of him again.

She stiffened beneath his touch. He half expected her to bolt, but she didn't. For appearances' sake, most likely. Might be she thought if she made a show of resistance, all three Basques would unload their cartridges on him.

He relaxed. Some.

Relaxing made him aware of how natural it felt to stand beside her, his hand on her hip, learning the soft curve on this part of her body—

And where did *that* thought come from?

He snatched his hand away.

"I'm not here to hurt anyone," he said firmly. "I need her help. Nothing more."

"I think it is best we are left alone, Mr. Wells." Trey had never known Gabirel Vasco to be anything less than respectful, but now, his expression showed how Trey's presence troubled him. "Please go."

"You're looking better," Trey told him, not budging and going for a change of subject. "Better than when I saw you last."

He meant it. At least now the man had the strength to walk. His cheeks weren't so pale, either.

But sadness drooped his eyes, showing the grief from the sheep he'd lost, his worry over Mikolas, too, and the thoughts pulled a good dose of sympathy through Trey.

"He's better because of Dr. Shehan's good care. Isn't that right, Papa?"

Zurina pinned Gabirel with a pointed look, which Trey took to mean her father needed to be reminded it was through Trey's arranging that he received medical treatment. Trey didn't want the gratitude—nor did he want the man to be an enemy. They'd always had a decent working relationship.

"He is not wanted here, Zurina." The third man waggled the barrel of his rifle. "He is trouble we do not need."

Her dark head whipped toward him. "Deunoro, you're wrong. He has news about Mikolas. *That* is why he's here."

For a moment, no one moved.

"Mikolas?" Gabirel croaked, lowering his weapon.

"Yes. But first, it's only right that I make introductions so Trey—Mr. Wells—knows who he is talking to," Zurina said curtly. "Already, we waste too much time."

Trey took the initial step toward the heavy-set one, standing in the middle, and extended his hand.

"Trey Wells," he said.

"He is my uncle, Benat Ibarran. Papa's brother and Ander's father," Zurina said.

The Basque made no attempt to return Trey's handshake. Gabirel elbowed him in the ribs. Finally the rifle lowered, and he reciprocated.

"I know who you are," Benat muttered.

Zurina indicated the third Basque. "Deunoro Ugarti, my cousin on my mother's side."

The sun had etched lines into Deunoro's craggy face, making him appear older than his years. Was an easy guess the man herded sheep for a living, and the suspicion directed at Trey meant his resentment for cattlemen was deep-seated. The massacre of the Vasco flock didn't help matters any.

But Deunoro took Trey's hand, muttered something between barely moving lips and shook with a firm grasp. Trey considered the gesture a victory of sorts. They'd all made it clear as rain he was an outsider. The enemy. He didn't much know if the feud would ever get better.

Still, he was here, and they hadn't shot him yet. Could be they were finally beginning to understand that Trey had no intention of stirring up trouble, that they needed each other to find Mikolas and Allethaire.

"Let us go into the cabin," Gabirel said. "We will talk more there."

"Not much time for talking," Trey said and handed him the ransom note. "When you see this, you'll understand why."

Gabirel took the note with his good arm. Reading it, he paled and made a fast Sign of the Cross. "God help us."

"What is it, Gabirel?" Benat took the note. He sucked in a loud, shocked breath.

"What? What?" Deunoro snatched the paper. The next moment, his features crumpled, and he beat at his chest with his fist. "This cannot be!"

"The words lie!" Gabirel swayed, as if he hovered on a faint. "My son would never do anything so terrible as this. Kidnap a woman? Demand money for her? Threaten to kill her? Never!"

Zurina hurried toward him and slipped her arm through his. "He writes his own name, Papa. It's the same as it has always been. There's an explanation, but we just don't know it yet. Come. Can you walk? We must get you inside so you can rest." She gently, firmly, turned him and coaxed him back to the cabin. "Uncle Benat, Deunoro. Come with us. Another glass of wine, and you'll feel better. Think better. Come."

She was the rock in their storm. Trey marveled at

her control, her logic, her ability to care for them in their shock and grief.

Like lost ducks, they followed. Knowing they didn't much care what he did, Trey followed, too.

"I must find him." Gabirel sounded frantic. "I must hear with my own ears how he comes to demand this money."

"Papa, he didn't kidnap Allethaire. We were there, remember? We *know* he didn't."

"Mikolas would never hurt us." Gabirel spoke with vehemence. "We are his family. He knows how important the sheep are to us."

"Of course, he does." Not once had she doubted it. Zurina squeezed his arm in assurance.

"Who is this Woodrow Baldwin? Who else is with him? What spell do these men cast on my son that makes him do this evil?"

"I don't know, Papa. I wish I did."

Zurina threw a glance back at Trey. If she thought he had any insight into the man's identity, she thought wrong.

"I'll do what I can to find them, Gabirel," he said from his place at the end of their line. "I've got a posse rounded up who want answers, too. Just like you do."

"You won't find Mikolas easily." Zurina dismissed his plan. "Do you not think we have searched every place he could be?"

Her certainty of his failure rankled. "He's *some-where*, Zurina."

They reached the cabin, and keeping a careful hold on her father, she pulled the door open. "Watch your step, Papa."

The four of them went inside. Not invited, Trey held back. He wasn't sure he'd be welcome if he entered the privacy of the Vasco home; he was all but sure no cattleman had ever stepped foot over the threshold before.

Impatience rolled through him. He couldn't glean information if he was left out of their conversation, and without information, he'd never find Alle-thaire.

He couldn't leave until he spoke with the Basques. With Zurina. He'd give her a few minutes, then knock on the door, demand to be let in. *Make* them talk to him.

He heaved a frustrated sigh, hooked a thumb in his hip pocket and slid a glance around the place. Zurina's home was small, for sure. Barely big enough for one person, let alone a family. Near as he could tell, she didn't have a husband in her life. He guessed she lived here with Gabirel, and since she'd never mentioned having a mother, Trey had to assume it was just the two of them.

He wouldn't let himself dwell on her not having a husband. Yet his thoughts did just that.

Dwelled on it.

He turned curious as to why no man had claimed her yet. She was beautiful. Spirited. Loving and strong. And those dark eyes of hers. Shiny, like black diamonds. Long, thick hair—how could any man resist wrapping the silky strands around his fist? Slide them slow and easy through his fingers?

His groin stirred with a slow, steady warmth that felt illicit. Unfair to Allethaire. She held no place in his heart, not anymore, but he corralled his lusty thoughts to something safer, nevertheless.

The yard.

Well-tended. The rough grass clipped even. A few straggly flowers popped up along the crude foundation, but it was a lone rosebush growing a few yards from the door that snagged his attention.

He never claimed to be a horticulturist, but this bush was finer than most. Obviously someone showered the thing with tender care. Pruned, full and thriving, the bush produced striking red blooms. So many loaded the prickly branches, they sagged under the weight.

The roses looked out of place here amidst the plainness. Every day, the Basques faced the challenges of living in the harsh hills. Raising sheep and eking out a mundane existence. They couldn't afford to be extravagant, but this rosebush was one exception.

For some reason, those deep red petals reminded him of Zurina. Beauty against plainness. As if she was destined for greater things, but denied them by the shackles of her heritage.

Helluva shame, for sure.

Giving into impulse, Trey went over and snapped off a stem. One of the nicest. Full of richly shaped petals.

The perfect rose.

A reminder of Zurina.

When he left, when he found Allethaire, when Woodrow and Mikolas accounted for their crimes, he would have it. A symbol from the time he'd known her.

"My father gave the bush to my mother when I was born."

Zurina's quiet voice yanked Trey from his ruminating. He turned.

She stood outside the cabin's door. "It cost him a fortune. He had it shipped all the way from New York."

Trey stood there, holding the stem, feeling stupid from being caught thieving something so frivolous. He twirled the rose between his fingers. "Do you mind?"

"Not at all. They're meant to be enjoyed." Her gaze lingered over the bush. "How Mama managed to keep the roses growing out here always amazed me."

"A labor of love."

"Yes." Zurina drew in a breath, sadly let it out

again. "She died earlier this spring. She would've loved seeing the roses in full bloom again."

Zurina's revelation startled him. The realization they'd lost a parent within weeks of the other, that her grief was as raw as his, turned his chest heavy with sympathy.

"I'm sorry," he said.

He hoped she knew he meant the words. His own mother died shortly after he was born, and his father never found another woman he deemed worthy enough for marrying, leaving Trey to grow up with only one parent. Zurina had had two. Still, he knew how mothers had a special closeness with their daughters.

Like fathers had with their sons.

"Thank you for saying so," she said quietly.

He forced his mouth to smile. "Reckon she's watching you from the Pearly Gates, making sure you water the bush for her."

Zurina's mouth curved, too. Sad still. "That would be like her, yes." She hesitated. "Allethaire told me your father was killed."

He swallowed. "Yes."

"A terrible thing."

"The worst."

He breathed in against a shaft of pain. The ugly and sharp reminder of how Sutton's life had been taken from him before his time.

Trey angled his head away and railed against

the unfairness. He hurt, and only revenge would ease it.

Yet here he was, squandering valuable time talking to Zurina. Delaying the score he was determined to settle, knowing full well the terms of that ransom note weren't going to change while he stood here with her.

"No one deserves to die from such violence—no matter how many sins he commits," she said, not looking at him.

An odd comment for her to make, he mused. And she voiced no condolences.

He expected as much from her. It seemed to be her way to show compassion like that.

But she merely opened the door. "My father wants to talk to you. Please come in."

A vague sense of disappointment swirled through Trey. Strange how he needed to hear her sympathy. To feel himself surrounded by her commiseration.

But he shook off the need. The weakness. He had more immediate matters to tend to. Like what to do with the rose in his hand.

He frowned.

"It's a shame the blooms will be wilted when you give them to her," Zurina said.

Before Trey could correct her, make clear he didn't intend to give it to Allethaire like she thought, Zurina went inside. For lack of a better idea, he made quick work of clearing the thorns, then stuffed the flower into his shirt pocket, hiding it from sight.

Trey pulled open the door. Once inside her cabin, he helped himself to a curious look around. Not much to see except for the table, stove and sideboard which took up most of the interior space. Across the room, brightly colored striped fabric curtained the openings to what would be the sleeping quarters. A picture of the Mother and Child hung on one wall; beneath it, several candles burned on a small polished table, the top of which was covered with a delicate-looking crocheted doily. In the corner stood a weaving loom and a basket with balls of yarn. The scent of fresh-baked bread hung in the air. Brewing coffee, too.

Zurina's tidy home had a welcoming feel. A woman's touch.

Hers.

Some of his unease lifted.

"Would you like a glass of wine?" she asked.

He preferred a cigarette. And since he'd never acquired a taste for wine, a cold beer if she had one. Which apparently she didn't.

"Coffee would be fine. Thanks," he said instead.

"I have just made some. Sit."

She pulled out the only available chair left at the table. Trey hoped the rickety thing would hold his weight.

He pulled off his hat. Sat carefully. The chair

proved sturdy, and he relaxed, then faced the three men staring at him.

A lesser man would've been intimidated, he decided, staring back at each one in turn. Their black-eyed glowers and knitted brows declared their resentment for him still ran strong.

Trey ignored their antagonism. The longer he dallied, the less time he had to track down Allethaire. The longer he stayed away from her, the more danger she was in.

He opened his mouth to start a serious discussion on how best to track down Mikolas—but Zurina slid a cup of steaming coffee in front of him, then added a plate heaped with thick slices of sourdough bread and a hunk of something pale.

His intentions withered. That hunk of something pale worried him.

He cleared his throat and shot a quick glance up at her, but it seemed she'd gotten real busy all of a sudden filling her father's glass with wine.

Trey didn't know if he should throttle her—or beg her mercy. She had to know she'd put him in one hell of a predicament.

He casually lifted his cup. Took a sip of the strong brew to buy himself some precious time. And watched her. *Willed* her to look at him.

After she poured for her uncle, then moved over to her cousin, she finally gave up ignoring him.

Their glances met.

What the hell is this? his demanded.

Her brow arched. *What? You don't like it?*

Like it, hell. She knew damn well he wouldn't like it.

Whatever it was.

She leaned over the table and positioned the almost-empty wine bottle in the center. Her nearness filled his senses. Her womanly scent, too, and the warmth of her body.

"You'll find the sheep's milk cheese delicious, Mr. Wells," she said smoothly. "It's called 'Manchego,' and it's Uncle Benat's specialty."

"That so?"

Her uncle nodded gravely. "My grandfather first made it in Spain, where the sheep lived on the dry plains. I come to America, and I make it here. I age it. Six months. When it is ready, I smear the cheese with olive oil, so that it tastes very Mediterranean. Like it is from Spain."

"That so?" Trey said again, feigning interest.

Zurina strolled past him and leaned a slender hip against the sideboard, crossed her arms and regarded him with a challenging arch to her brow.

"Try it, Mr. Wells," she purred.

She knew damn well no self-respecting cattleman would eat anything that smacked of sheep, and Trey had already done more than his share of tolerating the woollies. He let them graze on Wells range, hadn't he? Sun River Valley.

He drew the line at eating sheep.

Yessiree.

He smirked inwardly. He knew the game Zurina played. And she played, expecting him to refuse.

He took another sip of coffee. Swirled it in his mouth. Debated the merits of letting her win. Debated, too, the consequences from refusing while three of her strong-willed, cattleman-hating, trigger-happy relatives watched.

Would they refuse to help him find Mikolas? Woodrow? Allethaire? Would they have suggestions where Trey should look but out of spite keep them to themselves?

Trey set his coffee down. He couldn't risk it. Damn it to hell, he didn't dare.

He gathered his willpower. Buried his pride— *cattleman's* pride. He broke off a chunk of the pale Manchego-or-whatever-it-was-called and threw it in his mouth. By the time he swallowed, it took all the muscles in his face to keep from showing his revulsion.

The cheese had a potency to it, all right. A strange nutty *sheep* taste.

"It's even better with wine," Zurina murmured, handing him a fresh glass of that, too.

Calling himself all kinds of a coward, he snatched it from her and tossed back a gulp.

Both the sheep cheese and Basque wine slid down his throat and into his belly.

There. He'd done it.

Uncle Benat nodded his approval.

Deunoro leaned back in his chair with a slow, satisfied grin.

Gabirel visibly relaxed with a sigh of admiration.

And Zurina gifted him with a languid smile that tilted his world and warmed his blood and made him think of long, hot nights.

He knew, then, he'd passed their test.

Chapter Ten

Watching him, knowing how much it cost him, something went soft inside Zurina's heart.

Trey showed some of the fairness Papa had always associated with him. As a cattleman, Trey had met her family halfway. He'd been willing to step through the door into the sheepman's world.

But not too far.

She hid her amusement. It hadn't been easy for him to eat the cheese. To drink the wine. Doing so had forced him to commit an act most cattlemen considered unspeakable.

But he'd done it. With only a slight bruising to his pride.

"My son is a good man, Mr. Wells." Papa's voice sounded strong in his conviction, and all eyes swung toward him. Including Zurina's. "Why he puts his name on the ransom note is a mystery to me."

"To all of us," Uncle Benat added.

"He claims to have the woman, Allethaire. If it is true, and we must believe it is so, I know in my heart he has good reason to have her," Papa finished, looking somber.

"Can't think of any reason that might be good, Gabirel." Trey speared him with a hard glance. "Holding a defenseless woman against her will is wrong. Demanding money for her makes it worse. He's paired up with Woodrow Baldwin, who's rustling WCC cattle. And we can't forget what Woodrow has done to your sheep." Trey leaned back in his chair with the grimness of a judge who'd just pronounced a death sentence. "Both of them must be stopped."

Zurina had never known her brother to act like this. Devious and calculated and greedy. Hearing Trey talk about him, as if he were a criminal of the worst kind, was like hearing about a complete stranger.

Mikolas was hurting and angry. She suspected he was feeling lost, too, his identity taken after he'd learned what Sutton Wells had done. If she had to make excuses for her brother, it would be those.

Yet they didn't make what he'd done acceptable and right. For once, she had to agree with Trey.

Mikolas had to be stopped.

"I'm here because I want him found." Trey spoke each word in a clipped, tight voice, but Zurina heard the veiled plea in the words as well. "I'm hoping you can help."

"We have been talking about that." Deunoro nodded gravely.

"Helping you," Uncle Benat clarified.

"We think we know how."

Zurina's glance swung to her father in surprise. "You do?"

"How?" Trey demanded.

"We have thought of one place he might be." Looking grim, Papa rubbed his chin, as if even now he considered it a long shot.

"Where?" Zurina asked.

For days, weeks, she had racked her brain thinking. She'd imagined herself in Mikolas's body, feeling his feelings, what he might do, where he might go.

No one had seen him. No one had heard from him. She'd failed at every turn, and so had her father.

"Rogers Pass," he said.

Slowly she straightened.

She'd not been there in years, not since she was a young girl. The last time had been terrible, so frightening she shouldn't have forgotten.

Rogers Pass. *Rogers Pass.*

Why hadn't she thought of it before?

Why hadn't anyone?

"It is a terrible place for the Vascos," Deunoro said sadly. "The journey very difficult."

"Not even the sheep will go there." Uncle Benat shook his head.

Trey's glance jumped between them. "So why would Mikolas? Woodrow?"

"It's the perfect hideout." Zurina's certainty grew, along with the pounding of her heart. "Very isolated. Mikolas would know this. He would *know* they would be safe."

Trey frowned his skepticism. "I've never heard of it."

"Because there is little grass for the cattle, and it's high in the mountains," Zurina said.

"Only our family knows of it," Deunoro said.

A shadow darkened her father's features. "And fur trappers."

"It is worth a try, is it not?" Uncle Benat demanded. "To look for him in the pass?"

"Yes." Zurina's feet began to move, past Trey's chair. Past Deunoro's. "I will go right away."

Trey's head came up. "What?"

Papa appeared stricken. "'Rina, are you sure?"

"Yes, Papa."

"What happened there—"

"Was a long time ago." She flung back the curtain to her small room and went inside.

"If it's as dangerous as you all think, then Zurina has no business riding out," Trey said.

She envisioned him scowling at the other three as

she yanked open the drawer to her old dresser and pulled out her woolen sweater.

"I can do it," she called out.

"Give me directions, and I'll go myself. With the posse," he called back.

She snorted and didn't care if he could hear. "You would only get lost with them."

"Tell her she stays, Gabirel."

On the other side of the drape, Trey's voice rumbled with command, and who was he to tell her father what to do? Who was he to say what *she* could do?

Zurina yanked back the curtain and poked her head out. "You want to go by yourself, Trey? You want to get lost? Fine. It doesn't matter to me. If Mikolas is there, I'll find him first."

She pulled back again and dropped a pair of thick socks onto the sweater, kicked off her sandals and went for her ankle boots.

"You're not strong enough to be left alone, Gabirel," Trey protested. "Do you have someone to care for you if Zurina takes off?"

Zurina stilled. *That* she hadn't thought of. In her haste and hope to find Mikolas, she'd forgotten how fragile Papa was.

"My wife will watch over him." Uncle Benat spoke up quickly. "Neria will take good care of him, and we do not live far from here."

Zurina blew out a big breath of relief. She trusted

her aunt Neria implicitly. Papa was sure to get better under her watchful eye. Besides, he was already on the mend. He wouldn't be too much of a burden.

"Thank you, Uncle Benat," she called out and pulled on her socks and boots.

"Hunting down these outlaws is work not meant for a woman." Trey's tone had grown hard. A little desperate. "It's dangerous, it's tough and she could get hurt."

"She knows where to go, Mr. Wells," Papa said.

"Send a man in her place."

"Who is not out with their flocks?" Uncle Benat asked. "Gabirel is too sick. Me, I am too old."

"And I have never been to this Rogers Pass. I would get lost, too," Deunoro said, regret in his voice.

"Zurina is the only one who can do this," Gabirel said firmly. "There is no one else."

The responsibility of what she must do weighed heavily upon her shoulders. She would not think of what had happened there, all those years ago, in that tiny cabin hidden in the woods. If he could, Papa would spare her the journey. The memories. Anyone in her family would.

But she relished a new opportunity to find Mikolas. To help Allethaire. To exact justice on Woodrow Baldwin for destroying the Vasco flock.

Zurina vowed to do it all, with or without Trey's help.

* * *

As much as Trey hated to admit it, coming up here to see Zurina had turned into a big mistake.

He riveted a hard stare on that curtain. He had to find a way to convince her to stay put. It was clear something had happened to Zurina at Rogers Pass. No one was saying what, and why the men in her family would consent to her returning he couldn't comprehend, but her place was here, in her home, taking care of her father.

Where she'd be safe.

She was just going to have to accept the fact Rogers Pass was no place for her. She'd have to learn, too, he had every intention of hunting down Mikolas without her.

He didn't need Zurina's help anymore. His destination changed the circumstances, and he needed the *posse's* help more.

Impatience rolled through him at being forced to wait until she emerged from her room when every muscle in his body ached to march in there and make her stay behind.

He leaned back in his chair. A gully-washer of worry poured through him for all Allethaire was going through while he sat here, doing nothing but be a victim of propriety. Allethaire wouldn't be in danger if it wasn't for him, and he refused to make the same mistake with Zurina.

The curtain swished open. Zurina emerged from

her room with a determined stride that took her straight past him to the sideboard. Trey noted the sweater she carried, the rolled blanket under her arm, and from the way she threw bread and cheese into a towel, she'd be out the door in moments.

He stood. "Zurina, listen to me."

She ignored him. "I'll bring the rifle, Papa. And extra cartridges. Give me all you have."

"God save us, Zurina, if you have to shoot your own brother," Gabirel said, making a Sign of the Cross. But he rose with Benat's assistance and shuffled toward a shelf in the corner of the kitchen.

"I will saddle the mare for you, Zurina," Deunoro offered.

"Thank you." He headed outside, and she cast Trey an imperious glance. "It's not Mikolas I'd shoot, but the man with him. Woodrow Baldwin."

Trey scowled. "You're not going to shoot anyone, Zurina. When it comes time for reckoning, let me do it. Or the posse."

"And where is your posse, eh?" She pulled the towel's four corners together into a secure knot.

"Not far," Trey said. At the time, his reasoning to have them lay low had been sound—to keep from alarming the Basques while looking for Zurina. "But—"

"You want to go down to them? Fine. I'll leave without you. Uncle Benat, please bring Aunt Neria to me. There are some instructions I must give her."

Trey gritted his teeth. "Damn it, Zurina."

She took the box of shells her father handed her, added the old Henry rifle and her gear and strode toward the door with determined thumps of her boot heels. "I'll be right back, Papa."

Benat hustled his girth after her, and Trey moved to follow.

"Mr. Wells."

He halted at the sound of Gabirel's voice behind him. It was just the two of them left in the cabin, and Trey chafed at the delay.

"When you go to Rogers Pass, I will kill you if you hurt her," Gabirel said slowly.

He stood with one hand on the back of the chair, steadying himself, but he faced Trey with shoulders squared and his black eyes cold with warning.

Trey's gaze narrowed. "Damn you for thinking I would."

"Your father was a hard man. He took what he wanted. You are like him in many ways."

Trey found truth in the words. Sutton Wells rose to power as a wealthy cattleman by making plenty of enemies during the climb up. Now that he was gone, Trey intended to hold the reins to the WCC empire with the same hard-fisted grip as his father once held them.

"I'll take that as a compliment," he growled.

"It was not meant as one."

As a sheepherder, he wouldn't harbor any love

for Sutton Wells. Trey knew it. Accepted it. But he'd long valued his relationship with Gabirel Vasco for the honesty and respect they kept between them.

Gabirel's hand fisted. "My daughter is a beautiful woman, Mr. Wells—"

"And she's safe with me. You have my word on it. I promise you I'll watch out for her. She's got no business traipsing through dangerous country. As her father, you should know it and forbid her from going."

"She goes for me. She goes because it is all we have left."

Trey's brow arched. "Of your pride, you mean."

Gabirel stiffened. "It would be no different for you."

Trey had to give him the point. He made a reluctant nod of concession. "Under different circumstances."

"The night the sheep were killed, Zurina and I, we were defenseless. We could not fight back, and now we have been shamed as sheepherders. We have been destroyed." Gabirel took a moment to breathe, to swallow. "We must find out who did this to us. We must learn why."

"I'll find out for you."

"Only Zurina knows where to go."

"Damn it, Gabirel. She can tell me how to get there."

"And if you cannot find the exact place? Then you lose valuable time."

Trey recalled the terms of the ransom note and gritted his teeth. *Dusk. Tomorrow. Wolf Creek.* He was losing valuable time, all right. Arguing a decision neither Zurina nor Gabirel intended to change.

He swung around and headed out the door, not caring that it slammed shut behind him or that he'd not told Gabirel goodbye. Trey's searching glance found Zurina leading a horse from her poor-excuse-for-a-barn, her cousin barely visible inside.

Trey strode toward her, down the long side of the cabin and planted his feet in front of her. Her stride never faltered, and their gazes clashed. Her chin lifted to a defiant angle.

She would've kept on walking past him with her impertinent nose in the air if Trey hadn't hooked his arm around her waist and stopped her. In one swift move, he half-carried, half-spun her out of her stride and held her prisoner against the back of the cabin, then pressed his knee between her thighs to keep her there.

He heard the fear in her quick inhalation and couldn't much blame her for it. He wasn't in the habit of rough-handling women, but Zurina had long since stopped listening to any reasoning he attempted to make.

"I'm not going to hurt you," he growled.

She smacked both palms against his chest and

pushed hard to free herself, but Trey held his ground.

"Is this how a cattleman acts to get what he wants?" she hissed.

He gripped her shoulders to stop her wriggling. "Only when he's driven to it."

"Get away from me!"

"Settle down, Zurina. Just listen, will you?"

No one could see them here behind the cabin, but Trey knew it wouldn't be long before someone in her family came looking for her. And it sure as hell wouldn't do for them to see her like this, wedged between him and the back of the cabin against her will.

But he didn't move away.

Not yet.

"Tell me where you think Mikolas might be hiding out," he commanded, his voice low to keep from carrying. "Tell me how to get there."

"It has been a long time."

Which meant what? That she wasn't sure? That she could lead him on a wild-goose chase when he'd lost too much time already?

His eyes narrowed. "Try."

She glared up at him. "Why should I have you do what I must do for myself?"

"You have no idea what you're up against, Zurina."

"Mikolas is my brother."

"And he's with a gang who murdered your sheep."

She stiffened. Her throat moved, and Trey knew his point hit home. A raw, aching spot deep inside her.

"Let me go instead," he rumbled. His grip lessened over her shoulders. "I'll do this for you."

Her eyes latched onto his, as if she struggled to deem him worthy of her trust. Or her hate.

She studied him so long, so hard, Trey almost forgot why they were here, behind her cabin. Hidden from the men who wanted only to protect her from those they perceived as their enemies.

Cattlemen, at the top of their lists.

His body took note of hers, an awareness that had always been there, he suspected. From the moment he first saw her, beside her burned-out wagon. A simmering of his senses that if he wasn't careful, if he didn't rein his attraction in, could very easily boil over into something it shouldn't.

Like now.

A slow heat stirred in his groin, and his thigh registered the feel of hers pressed against him. Their shape, slim and toned. Their warmth through her skirt. How they would feel spread and lifted and curled around his hips…

He shouldn't be thinking of her like this, but God help him, he was. He had only to move closer, inches closer, to feel the rounded globes of her breasts against his chest. He had only to lower his head…

Her mouth drew him. More than anything else, it was her mouth. To taste the softness of her lips, to discover their shape, trace them with his tongue, give in to this damned crazy ache to kiss her hard and long and never stop.

"What are you afraid of, Trey?" she asked.

Though her voice whispered between them, the sound jarred his burgeoning lust. He needed a moment to focus.

To think.

What are you afraid of?

Afraid?

Of being left alone with a beautiful woman up at Rogers Pass? Someone besides Allethaire?

Is that what it was?

Fear?

He drew back. Realization turned him cold. Fear of the truth. Maybe. That he didn't love Allethaire and never would. And it was being with Zurina, just the two of them without the distraction of the posse, that scared the hell out of him.

Zurina shook up his world, for sure. Turned it crazy sideways. This Basque woman who had no more a part in his life than he had in hers.

She was different from Allethaire. That's all. Just different. So she intrigued him. Made him want her in ways he shouldn't. Lusty, blood-warming, *forbidden* ways.

But she made him determined to protect her, too. Inspired in him a need to help her and Gabirel, to right the wrongs done to them both.

"Trey?"

Zurina repeated his name with that same whisper in her voice. God, he loved the sound of it. Sultry and easy. As if she'd spoken his name a thousand times before. Intimate as a lover's.

His brain cleared. His senses sharpened. He eased his grip over her shoulders.

Her hands still lay against his chest, but they didn't seem so determined to push him away. Not anymore. Instead, they rested with gentle familiarity, as if they belonged there. Close to his heart.

Hell.

If being afraid got him to feeling poetic, too, then he'd best get to facing his fears head-on. Beat them down to a pulp, so he could get on with his life. And Zurina could get on with hers.

"Only thing I'm afraid of, sweetheart, is not finding that brother of yours," he drawled, though a hard edge had crept into his voice. "If you're going to help me do it, then you'd best mount up in a hurry." His mouth quirked at the irony. "Or I'm leaving without you."

She pulled back, clearly surprised at his change

of heart. But she didn't ask questions, and he didn't give answers.

Mostly because he didn't have any.

But Trey figured by the time things were all said and done, he'd have all the answers they needed.

Chapter Eleven

"Well?"

Woodrow drew up at the rope corral where Mikolas stood waiting, looking as touchy as a teased snake.

"He's got the ransom note," Woodrow said and dismounted.

"You sure?"

"Saw him take it."

"At the line camp?"

That had been the initial plan. To leave the note at the nearest WCC line camp so it'd be found by one of the Wells' cowboys, then delivered to Trey. Woodrow had decided it'd be safer that way.

But the line camp had been deserted, and Woodrow didn't want to take a chance on days going by before the note was found. He'd helped himself to the cattle instead, never expecting to run into Trey and the posse in his flight back to the hideout.

"No." Woodrow lifted his hat, wiped the grime from his forehead, slapped the hat back on again. "Paid some sheepherder's kid to give it to him."

Mikolas stilled. "What sheepherder's kid? That wasn't the plan."

"I had to make a new one, all right?" Impatience sparked through Woodrow like a lit firecracker. "It worked, so what difference does it make if I changed the plan?" God, he'd gotten tired of Mikolas's whining. He craved a drink. And he was starved. "Have the bitch make me something to eat."

"She doesn't cook."

Woodrow's lip curled in disgust. Which didn't surprise him. Allethaire Gibson was used to being catered to and waited on, just so she could be lazy her entire filthy-rich life.

Well, that was going to change.

He found her near the fire, sitting on a boulder jutting from the ground. If only big-brother Trey could see her now, with her hair tangled and that expensive black dress of hers dusty and creased with wrinkles. Even from here, Woodrow could tell her eyes were red and swollen. Half from crying, the other from swilling too much brandy.

Woodrow would bet his eyeteeth Trey didn't know his precious intended was a drunk, and Woodrow looked forward to enlightening him.

Soon. Very soon.

Until then, Allethaire was going to have to fall off

her high horse, and Woodrow was going to be the one to give her a good, strong push.

He strode toward her with anticipation in his blood. She held a black kitten in her lap. *His* black kitten. A stray he'd taken from the WCC barn the night he'd stolen his Appaloosa.

"Give my kitty to me," Woodrow snarled and snatched the little feline away. "Now get up and make me supper."

"Damn you." She made no move to obey and showed more vim and vinegar than he'd seen from her so far. "Fix your own supper. I'm not your mother."

Woodrow froze. His sweet mama was nothing like this bitch. Mama loved him. She'd always loved him, even when no one else did.

Including his own father.

Mama would've made him supper. Whatever he wanted, with what little she had, and how dare this hoity-toity bitch defame the one person he'd ever truly loved?

In pure, unadulterated rage, Woodrow drew up and backhanded her. The blow toppled her from the rock. She cried out, covered her face with her hands and curled into a tight, sobbing ball.

"Leave her alone!" Mikolas yelled.

But Woodrow went for her again, his rage unquenchable. Before he could grab her scrawny, pampered arm and yank her up from the dirt, Mikolas clamped a hand on his shoulder and shoved him back.

Woodrow nearly lost his grip on the kitten. Nearly lost his balance, too. And if Mikolas hadn't pulled out his shooting iron, Woodrow would've gone after him next.

"Leave her alone," Mikolas shouted. "You hear, Woodrow? The score we have to settle has nothing to do with her. It's Trey, damn you. Trey."

"I'm not putting up with her sass anymore!" Breathing hard, Woodrow stroked the kitten's back, furiously, again and again, soothing the tiny creature. Soothing himself. "There's other ways of getting what's coming to us. We don't need her."

"Then why don't you let me go?" Allethaire choked back a sob and pushed herself to a sitting position. Tears streaked her cheeks and smeared the blood streaming from her lip. "Or better yet, just shoot me." She looked like a wild woman with her wide, reddened eyes. Her hair a rat's nest. "Shoot me so I don't have to look at your disgusting face." Her voice rose to a screaming pitch. "Shoot me like you shot the sheepdog. Or set me on fire. I don't care anymore. I don't care."

Mikolas stared, first at Allethaire. Then at Woodrow. "What sheepdog? What fire?"

"She's talking crazy," Woodrow said, turning careful fast. "Don't pay any attention to her."

Instinct told him things had gone precarious. Mikolas being part Basque meant he was partial to sheep, and Woodrow had never told him what he'd done to kidnap Allethaire. At least, not all of it.

"Gorri," she said. "That's what they called the dog. Gorri."

Mikolas went white.

"He didn't deserve to be shot." Her dirty face crumpled, and she started crying again. "He was just an innocent little dog."

"What did you set on fire?" Shaking, pale, Mikolas took a step toward him. "A wagon? A sheepherder's wagon?"

"She's lying," Woodrow snarled. "I didn't set fire to anything."

"Yes, he did." Allethaire's watery gaze jumped between them. "He shot out their lantern, and it shattered."

"Whose lantern?" Mikolas leaped toward Woodrow and grabbed the front of his shirt. "Whose damn lantern, Woodrow?"

"Lamb-lickers, that's who! Stinking lamb-lickers!"

"Zurina's, I think." Allethaire sat very still, as if she realized the importance of the information pouring out of her. "And her father. He got shot, too. And his sheep. Lots of his sheep, and—"

Mikolas's yell drowned out the rest of her words, and he slammed his fist into Woodrow's jaw. Pain exploded in Woodrow's head, and he sprawled backward, into the dirt. His bones rattled; he lost hold of the black kitty. Then, Mikolas was there, on top of him, fist swinging, and Woodrow swore, swinging back.

Suddenly Reggie appeared and pulled Mikolas off him, holding him prisoner with a gun pressed to his back.

Woodrow, breathing hard, jaw throbbing, glowered up at both of them.

"Zurina is my sister," Mikolas panted, straining against Reggie's grip. "Gorri is our dog, and Gabirel is my father, and—"

"No," Woodrow roared. "No, he's not your father. Sutton is. Was." The harsh reminder echoed over the camp. No one moved. No one spoke. "You forget you're a Wells, Mikolas?" he rasped, calmer. "You're not a sheepherder no more, brother. You're going to be a cattleman, a *rich* cattleman, as soon as Trey pays up."

For a long moment, Mikolas didn't move.

Woodrow held his breath. As much as he hated to admit it, he needed Mikolas in his plan to blackmail Trey for Allethaire. Power in numbers and all that. Because Trey was powerful, too powerful, to fight alone.

"Yeah," Mikolas said finally. The fight seemed to drain from him. "Sure."

Reggie released him.

Woodrow sat up.

But the damage had been done.

He didn't trust Mikolas anymore.

* * *

Zurina had barely entered her teen years the last time she headed this way, toward Rogers Pass, but it felt like only yesterday. A lush but prickly blanket of juniper, spruce and Douglas fir draped the foothills of the Rockies. Plenty of crisp, cool air filled her lungs. To the east, the mountains took on the remarkable shape of a giant man sleeping along the horizon, making him appear at peace beneath a sky so sprawling with blue, who could tire of admiring it?

Yet the danger of what lay ahead, or at least the potential for it, overshadowed the pristine beauty. Certainly the memory of what she'd gone through that terrible day when she'd come within inches of losing her life.

She banked the memory. It was more important to think of Mikolas instead. To hope and pray he was there, hiding out near the pass. That he had Allethaire with him, and she was safe.

And of course, Woodrow Baldwin. The man who Zurina despised most of all. The one she blamed for crushing her dreams for a new and better life. One that would give her respectability as a sheepherder's daughter in a cattleman's world. Woodrow had all but stolen her money, too, when he killed the Vasco flock. He'd stolen the comfort her father deserved and the joy she craved in having a new house.

Worse, he'd turned her brother into someone he wasn't.

Zurina was afraid to think of what would happen if she failed to find them. If this journey ended as a wild-goose chase. Valuable time would be lost. And where could they possibly look next?

She couldn't think of failure. She must think only of success—and of the confrontation sure to ensue when she arrived.

Well, she would be glad to have Trey with her then, despite her original intentions to journey without him. Trey would be a formidable ally, a strong force in reaping justice for the crimes committed against them both.

From under her flat-brimmed hat, she studied him riding beside her, and the tiniest of flutters formed in her belly. He sat the saddle with power. With ease. With an unassuming strength she found damnably... appealing.

He didn't appear to notice her staring, and she dared to continue. He seemed more intent on studying the land around him, as if he readied himself for anything unexpected.

His mind would be absorbed, too, with his intended. Allethaire. He'd be missing her, wanting her back in his arms, looking forward to showering her face with happy, relieved kisses.

The thought painted a vivid image of the two. Sharing happy kisses. And a burning ache formed inside Zurina, so deep, so sudden, she could barely breathe.

She yanked her glance away and steeled herself against this illicit longing for what would never be. A man like Trey Wells loving her, a lowly sheepherder's daughter.

Pah! Those silly husband dreams again. Zurina gritted her teeth. It was more important to worry over how he would react when he learned Mikolas was his half brother.

Zurina dreaded the moment. A cattleman of his standing would only be shamed beyond measure.

Of its own accord, her gaze found him again. Lingered over the straight line of his nose, the square cut of his jaw, the proud thrust of his chin. Trey Wells wore his pride and influence like a king wore his royal cloak, and she suspected she could watch him, just soak the sight of him in, for days on end.

"Have I sprouted horns, woman?" he asked. His glance slid toward her, then. Slow and knowing. "Or have I turned green all of a sudden?"

She started guiltily that he'd caught her staring, but she found enough composure to give him a cool smile.

"I rather think the horns would suit you," she retorted, lifting her hands and spreading them wide. "Big longhorn ones."

"Yeah?" A side of his mouth lifted. "Better horns than a woollyback, I guess."

Another time, she would've taken grave offense. But the coppery glint in his eye revealed his teasing, and this time, at least, she let her defenses slide.

"You're a cattleman through and through, aren't you, Mr. Wells?" she asked, swinging her head with a haughty sniff.

"Yep." He let out a long, satisfied sigh. "Born and bred."

Mikolas had been born a Wells, too, she thought, but bred as a sheepman. How different their lives would be had they'd known each other and been raised as true brothers.

"I would've liked meeting you under different circumstances, Zurina." No longer did Trey's tone carry a teasing inflection. His expression revealed complete seriousness. "When being a cattleman didn't matter."

The steady pace of their horses rocked his body, but he rode with a fluid grace that showed how much he was at ease in the saddle.

"Yes," she said, her sigh heartfelt. "Me, too."

"It's hard—" he hesitated, as if choosing his words carefully "—it's frustrating for the cattleman when flocks of sheep destroy his range. The grass is too valuable."

"It's valuable for the sheep, too."

"But the sheep *kill* the grass, Zurina." He heaved a terse breath. "Then there's nothing left for the cattle.

They lose weight. We lose money. The quality of the beef goes down, and the whole market suffers."

"Yes." Many times, she had heard of these problems. "I have seen the range when the grass is eaten down to the roots. I understand how it is a bad thing."

"Worse than bad," he muttered. "It's intolerable."

"You must see the sheepman's side of it, Trey."

"When I see a range stripped of grass, I see all I need to see."

She glowered. "Will you let me explain?"

"I've heard every explanation there is by now, Zurina." A muscle moved in his jaw. "But I'll listen to yours."

"Thank you."

"You won't change my mind about how I feel."

"I don't expect it to be easy as that."

"All right. Go on, then. Give me your perspective."

At least he seemed willing to listen, and his urging for her to continue sounded genuine.

"When the grass is chewed down to nothing, then it's the sheepman's fault," she said. "He's careless. Lazy."

Trey grunted. But he said nothing.

"To save the grass, to respect it, he must keep moving the flock," she continued. "He can't let the sheep stay in one place too long."

"You think it's that simple?"

"I've seen it for myself, because that is how Papa tends our sheep in Sun River Valley. Every year, the grass grows thick there. The flock has all they need to eat."

"If that's so, then why did you leave, Zurina?"

His question hit home, and a ball of emotion welled in her throat. If only she hadn't wanted to leave the valley that day a lifetime ago, then so much damage wouldn't have been done. So many wouldn't have been hurt.

She avoided the intensity of Trey's regard and feared now would be the time when he would forever banish the Vasco flocks from Sun River Valley.

Except there was no Vasco flock. Not anymore.

But if there were…

"Papa didn't want to leave," she said in a voice hushed with regret. "I insisted because the flock needed water."

And because she'd been so persistent, Papa had given into her. Now Trey would have every right to revoke his agreement and forbid them from stepping foot in Sun River Valley again. By straying into forbidden range, Papa had betrayed Trey's trust.

But, of course, it didn't matter anymore. They couldn't graze a flock they didn't have.

"Zurina."

She couldn't bring herself to look at Trey just yet. He would only be secretly glad she'd lost so many sheep, even though he'd try not to show it.

"Look at me, Zurina."

She refused to ignore her pride and channeled her concentration on their surroundings. The clomp of the horses' iron hooves against the rocky ground indicated they'd ridden higher into the mountains. The air had grown cooler, the forest of pines denser.

"We must find a place to camp," she said, changing the subject with a brisk tone. "It'll turn dark up here soon. Very fast."

A moment passed. She could feel him watching her.

"There's a stream not far ahead," he said finally. "We'll bed down there."

Trey tugged on the reins and nudged his mount off the trail. Zurina took her time in following.

We'll bed down there.

Her hand found Papa's old rifle sheathed in its scabbard. Within easy reach. Her defense against Trey in case he tried to do something he shouldn't.

He was, after all, Sutton Wells's son. And Zurina could never forget the terrible act the man had committed against her mother.

Yet, a stubborn voice inside her insisted Trey was different. That he would never force himself on a woman like herself who lived and breathed sheep. He was too much of a cattleman, clear to his bones.

So why did that pique her feminine pride? That Trey might not find her appealing? Even if he *was* a cattleman? Even if he was beholden to another?

Zurina gritted her teeth at her fickle thoughts. Better that she be prepared to defend herself against the wild which roamed the slopes near Rogers Pass— wolves and mountain lions and oh, *grizzly bears*— than a powerful, stubborn cattleman.

She spurred her horse into a hasty trot, and by the time she reached him, he'd already dismounted near the water's edge. His chestnut quarter horse stood at the bank with his head dipped toward the crystal clear water. Stones glistened beneath the surface, and dappled sunlight winked over the shimmering current.

Trey stepped toward Zurina and held the bridle while she dismounted. Her sweater shielded her from the crispness in the air, but it wouldn't be long before the night turned downright cold.

She tilted her head back to see him. "If you take care of the horses, I'll gather some wood for a fire."

He nodded. "Sounds fair."

Yet she didn't move.

Neither did he.

The darkening copper-brown glints in his eyes held her captive. An awareness seemed to spring between them, as if now that they were out of their saddles, standing close together like this, the reality of the night ahead had settled in. The knowledge they were together, just the two of them and no one else.

His gaze wrapped around her and bound her in a

mysterious velvety grip. She wondered why he had this power over her. And how.

But he did. And he looked at her as if he wanted to swallow her whole.

Zurina refused to let him think she was weak enough to allow him. Or too vulnerable. She refused to let him know how much he affected her.

"Are you hungry?" she asked, reaching for the mundane. Something ordinary to shatter the spell.

"Getting there."

His voice carried a seductive thread, and her imagination leaped into a wild interpretation of what he might really mean.

Of what he didn't say.

She chastised herself for being so foolish, and the longer she stood here, the more foolish she'd get. She twisted to step around him, to seek refuge in the menial task of scavenging for firewood, but his lean fingers clasped her elbow. Preventing her.

"Not so fast, Zurina," he said.

She yanked free of his hold. Arched her brow in surprise and demand. "What do you want?"

His dark gaze roamed her face. "Stop blaming yourself for moving your sheep out of Sun River Valley."

He'd returned to the subject she'd wanted to avoid. Instant tears welled.

How had he known she blamed herself? Had her regret, her despair, been so obvious?

She would've stepped away to escape his perception, but his hand lifted, and his fingers curled around the back of her neck. She could no more flee him than sprout wings and fly, for the gentleness of his touch nearly proved to be her undoing.

"Oh, Trey," she whispered. "How can I not blame myself? Papa would never have left if it wasn't for me."

"What happened on the range wasn't your fault. No way could Woodrow have known you were going to be out there."

"But if Papa and I hadn't been, Woodrow wouldn't have killed the sheep."

"And he wouldn't have kidnapped Allethaire."

Zurina bit her lip. Her misery deepened. "No."

"He took advantage of an opportunity, Zurina. That's all."

Trey's thumb caressed the line of her jaw, and her knees went soft. Was she so hungry for his touch, his comfort, that he could affect her like this?

"A damned shame what happened," Trey said, his low voice grim. "I don't have the answers yet, but I will when I find him. One thing I know for sure. Woodrow has a vendetta against me. And he's using Allethaire to help satisfy it."

"Yes."

"So is Mikolas."

Zurina's eyes closed. "Yes."

Gently, firmly, Trey cupped the back of her head

and pulled her against him. She sank into his warmth, his strength. At the moment, she had none of her own.

"If you and Gabirel hadn't been camped along the Missouri with Allethaire, Woodrow would've found another way to hit at me," Trey rumbled. His lips moved against her hair. "It would've just been a matter of time."

Zurina sighed into his shirt. Clung to his logic and prayed that it was true. "Maybe."

Trey slid his hand up her spine. And down again. Slow, easy strokes that melted her worries. Bolstered her flagging spirits.

And made her much too aware of how much she needed to be with him. Absorb his strength. His warmth. To share her worries and fears.

"It's a helluva shame your sheep got caught in the middle of all this. I'm not sure how your brother fits in, either, Zurina, but neither he nor Woodrow will hurt Allethaire until they get their ransom money. Which means right now, until we meet them down at Wolf Creek tomorrow night, we're holding all the cards. They're just waiting for us to make the next deal."

Struck by how he included her in his plans, a strategy that went beyond her leading him to Rogers Pass, she drew back.

"We?" she asked softly.

"That's right." The coppery glints in his shadowed

orbs darkened like burned cinnamon. "You've got a score to settle, just like I do. We'll do it together." His thumb lifted. Traced the shape of her lips. They parted, and a craving to taste his skin, to draw his thumb into her mouth, welled in some secret part of her she'd kept banked for too long. "But first we have to call a truce."

Distracted by his bold caress, the way it inspired such forbidden, foolish longings, she had to scramble to follow his thinking.

"What kind of truce?" she murmured.

"No more squabbling about our differences."

"Cattle and sheep."

"From here on out, we're on equal terms."

"Hmm." Did he think it would be so easy?

"And one more thing."

At some point, her body had pressed itself to his. Thigh to thigh. Hip to hip. A new craving to feel more of him. Illicit and strong.

His arm pressed at the back of her waist, pulled her against the thickening of his groin.

"We seal our deal with a kiss," he said.

Chapter Twelve

Trey heard her quick inhalation of breath. Her slim body stiffened against him, and she would've pulled away if his arm hadn't banded tighter to keep her from it.

"What game are you playing with me, Trey?" she asked.

The slight knit to her brows hinted his suggestion had wounded her pride. He'd come to know her well enough to understand she'd think he only wanted to take advantage of her, considering they were all alone on this part of the mountain.

"No game." He made sure he sounded sincere. Because he was. "Asking you to kiss me is the same as asking you to trust me. I figure it's going to cost you plenty to kiss a cattleman, and if you can do that, we can work together on putting aside our differences."

"Really?" Her voice sounded cool. Skeptical.

"Going to be extra hard to track down Woodrow and Mikolas if we're thinking the worst of each other all the time."

She fiddled with the button on his shirt and seemed to make a pointed effort to keep from looking at him. "I don't think the worst of you so much anymore."

Well, then. He'd made some progress with her. She didn't hate him as much as she'd like to think.

The notion pleased him. She'd come to mean something to him, too.

Since she didn't seem inclined to push him away, he took the liberty of lowering his head. He nuzzled her hair—and thought of the wind on a spring day. She trembled, ever so faintly. A sign she wasn't unaffected by his touch, and that pleased him, too.

"C'mon, Zurina. Kiss me," he whispered and ran his tongue along the curve of her ear. "Just a little kiss to show you trust me."

Her head lifted to finally meet his glance; her fingers stilled over his button.

"What of Allethaire?" she asked quietly.

No one knew better than Trey how the woman everyone expected him to marry stood between him and Zurina and a whole wagonload of lust. But Allethaire had long since lost her place in his heart, in his life. Zurina wouldn't know that, but the realization had never been clearer to Trey than now, while he held her in his arms.

Allethaire could never be who he needed her to be. A woman who thought less of herself and more of those who needed her. A woman like Zurina—capable of fierce loyalty, immeasurable compassion, gentle nurturing. Who knew what it meant to be loved and who loved back with every fiber of her being.

Trey had witnessed the way Zurina loved. So had Gabirel, Mikolas, and all the other Basques who knew her. Without knowing she was, she made Trey realize what he'd missed—growing up without a female to take care of him, keep him important in her life—and it was a woman like her he wanted forever at his side.

"I'm not in love with her," he said firmly. Without hesitation. "I never have been."

Her brows shot up. "What?"

"I've already canceled our engagement."

Her breath caught. "You have?"

"So forget her."

"How can I?"

"Because I'm asking you to."

She blinked up at him in wary disbelief.

"One more thing to trust me about," he added.

From here on out, he'd walk a different road. One headed toward a future without Allethaire. And the kiss he wanted with Zurina wasn't going to happen while he stood here, rationalizing.

Trey knew Zurina was entitled to a full explanation, and he'd give her one.

Later.

The time had come to take what he wanted. What they both wanted.

Now.

A melding of trust. Of desire and need.

He tightened his embrace to bring her full against him and groaned at the feel of her slender, feminine body. He took her mouth with an explosion of hunger. Her lips, soft and full and a little tremulous, lit a hot, sweet fire in him too long banked. Too long restrained.

Zurina pressed into him, lifted her hands and curled her arms around his neck. As if her balance had shifted, as if she hovered on the brink of drowning in a sensation he alone made her feel. As if she cared nothing for what should be and what wasn't.

Before Allethaire, Trey had been with his share of women, but none affected him like this Basque beauty who knew little of society's airs and pretenses. Of bargains and marriages made for mutual benefit.

Zurina was freshness. Honesty and purity. Trey's need to experience more of her deepened, widened, demanded. His mouth opened over hers. His tongue glided over her lips in a persistent plea to satisfy the need. To quench his growing lust for more.

A tiny sound slid up from her throat. Acquiescence, primitive and pure. Her lips parted, and his tongue delved inward to the velvety depths, curled over hers, slid and rolled in a moist, hot dance that turned his breathing ragged and left her mouth swollen and wet.

Zurina drew back, dragged in air. "Trey. Oh God, Trey."

Was it guilt he heard when she spoke his name?

He angled his head and pressed ragged kisses along her jaw and into the curve of her neck. Distracting her from the guilt. The doubt. Erasing it all from her mind.

Her head tilted, her eyes closed. One hand fisted in his hair while the other clung to his shoulder. Her body fused itself to his. As if her bones had melted. As if her muscles had turned to mush.

"Zurina, let me make love to you." He sounded pathetically needy, even to his own ears. He was moving too fast, wanting too much, but there was no help for it. No stopping the lust raging inside him. "Now. Here, now."

"No, we must not." Despite her protest, she arched her neck, accommodating his journey to her collarbone, to taste her skin at the hollow of her throat. "We cannot, Trey."

Her words sounded wrenched. Reluctant. Decidedly firm. He might've admired her restraint if his own wasn't at the breaking point.

"I want to know you. All of you." His hand slipped beneath her thick sweater and found delicious warmth through her cotton blouse. Traveled over her ribs, too, and captured the perfect shape of a breast, loose inside her shift. His fingers flexed over the supple globe of flesh. Fondled, savored. "Let me, Zurina."

Her breath caught, and the tiny sound told him no man had ever had the privilege of touching her like he was touching her now. And if that wasn't trust…

His lust raged higher. He had only to shift their stances, take her with him down to the ground. Woo her with a sweet seduction that would fan the flames already burning in their blood.

"Stop, Trey."

She pushed against him and twisted out of his embrace. His lusty thoughts skittered to a halt.

"Zurina." He could scarcely manage more than a croaking of her name. "Zurina, sweetheart."

"I am not your sweetheart. Allethaire is." Her fingers shook while they righted her sweater. She took another step back from him, for good measure. "We are wrong to betray her."

The flames inside him sputtered. Sheer control kept him from reaching for her again. "I told you. I'm not going to marry her."

"Now you say so. And they are easy words to say, eh? When you're rutting like a pig for another woman."

He didn't appreciate the phrasing. "It's not like that, Zurina. And you know it."

"You got your kiss." Her throat moved with the

admission, as if she regretted giving into him. "Now you must not ask anything more of me."

Trey gritted his teeth and refused to make promises he had no intention of keeping. She strode away, into the shadows of the pines, leaving his ardor cooling while he tended the horses.

By the time supper was finished, Trey had had enough of her silence.

Either she was mad at him—or at herself. Or she was hurt, believing he'd taken advantage of her. Whatever her thinking, it'd be a long, cold night if he didn't clear the air between them.

He eyed her across the fire, noted how she seemed to look everywhere but at him. He washed down the last of his sourdough bread with coffee and set his plate down.

"Zurina."

Evidently she'd been so deep in her ignoring, the sound of his voice startled her. She visibly flinched.

"I'm right here. What do you want?"

"Don't be testy with me."

She glowered. "I'm only testy when I'm bothered by a high-handed cattleman. Like you."

He heaved a sigh. "Listen, Zurina. I admit I took the kiss too far."

She muttered something under her breath. In Euskara and likely scathing.

"I meant it when I said I'm not in love with Allethaire," he went on. "I would never have kissed you like I did if I *was* in love with her."

Her black eyes snapped back toward him. "Does she know you aren't?"

"She knows our marriage was a business arrangement, nothing more. The financial benefits weighed heavily in her favor."

"She speaks of you as her husband-to-be."

"Let me explain something to you."

Trey reached inside his shirt pocket for a cigarette. Found the wilted rose stem instead. He left it there and went for his coffee cup. After a slow sip, during which he strove to find the right words, he gripped the cup in both hands.

"My agreement to marry Allethaire cinched the deal on the hydro-electric plant her father wants to build on Wells land," he began.

Zurina appeared surprised. "Meaning?"

"Meaning in return, she would get a husband who would give her security for the rest of her life. When she lived in Minnesota, she was accustomed to living among folks with power and influence. Paris figured she'd get all that with me."

"The Wells Cattle Company is very powerful, yes." Zurina nodded in utmost seriousness. "But Allethaire didn't want you to love her first? Before she agreed to marriage with you?"

"Oh, she loved me all right. For my money."

Zurina clucked her tongue in disapproval. "I would

never marry a man I didn't love," she said firmly. "And I would not want him to marry me if he didn't love me more than anything."

"Not everyone can have the luxury of finding the perfect love out here, Zurina. Sometimes a man has to be practical. That hydro-electric plant is crucial to Montana's growth. Marriage to a beautiful, refined woman like Allethaire seemed a small price to pay to partner with her father on such an important deal."

"Then Allethaire shouldn't have agreed to your proposal. She doesn't love your ranch. And she doesn't love Montana."

"No. Nor was she willing to try."

Zurina studied him. She seemed to digest all Trey had told her. "I'm sorry."

"Don't be." He frowned. "It wasn't meant to be. I have no intention of moving to Minnesota."

"It was unfair to expect it of you."

"She wanted my father to run the ranch in my absence. But when he was murdered—" Trey halted on a wave of pain from the senseless act "—after he died, she knew there was no way I would ever leave."

"And so you argued on the day of your father's funeral. She left. She got lost, and that is how she found Papa and me."

"Yes."

Things went from bad to worse for Allethaire then.

Her kidnapping was something no one should ever have to go through.

Trey held himself responsible. No one else he could blame. If he'd been more sensitive to her demands, more understanding of her perspective, more willing to compromise, she wouldn't have gotten upset and left the ranch in a roaring tiff.

He could only hope she found the starch to survive her ordeal. Allethaire had grown up soft as pillow down from the pampering her parents had always given her. She had to be going through the hardest time of her life right now.

Worried, restless, he tossed aside his cup and stood. He left the warmth of the fire and strode over to the edge of the creek to think.

Moonlight splayed over the water. Cool air blew, and the silvery surface lapped gently against the rocky bank. Somewhere on the mountain, a coyote howled.

Another time, Trey would've found solace in a place like this, but not tonight. Not until he found Allethaire, settled his score with Woodrow and Mikolas—and avenged his father's murder.

And then there was Zurina. He'd known her for only a short time, and yet she'd burrowed her way under his skin. Into his blood. When everything was said and done, how would he walk away from her?

She was all woman. Vibrant and caring and beautiful. A man would be proud to call her his, to keep her in his heart, at his side, and in his bed.

What would it be like if he were that man? If he had Zurina all to himself—forever?

Behind him, footsteps crunched over the rocky ground, and his senses heightened to her approach. She halted beside him and crossed her arms over her chest to ward off the night's chill.

"I don't mind so much anymore that you kissed me like you did," she said.

His mouth curved. He declined to remind her she'd been a hot-blooded, willing participant to those kisses. He grasped her shoulders and pulled her against him.

"Then you won't mind me holding you like this to warm us both up, either," he murmured.

She came willing. Even laid her head against his chest, all familiar and easy.

"If we get an early start, we'll reach Rogers Pass by late morning, I think," she said against his shirt.

He rested his chin on the top of her head and thought of how much awaited them. None of it easy. "The earlier, the better then."

He sensed her hesitation. "I have something I must tell you before we get there."

"Yeah?"

Trey didn't much want to talk. Or think. It felt too good just standing here, holding her. Fantasizing about what it'd be like if she belonged to him. So he could hold her whenever he wanted.

"It's about Mikolas," she said.

He ran a hand up her spine and back down again through the soft wool of her sweater. He pressed his lips to her temple, thought again of how different she was from Allethaire.

"Can it wait?" he asked, procrastinating against the invasion of reality.

"No."

Her trouble-making brother would likely always be a sore spot between them. Trey couldn't think of a thing she could say that would change that.

But if she wanted him to listen, he would.

"What about him?" he asked.

Suddenly her head came up. "Did you hear that?"

He tensed. "Hear what?"

She pushed away. "Splashing."

Her head turned toward the creek in alarm. Trey raked a glance up one side and down the other.

"I don't hear anything," he said.

"Someone is in the water." She sprinted along the bank. "The splashing came from over there."

"I'll get my rope. Stay put, Zurina. Don't go running off. I'll be right back."

Damned strange to have someone—or something—splashing around out there this time of night. Trey didn't like having intruders so close, with him and Zurina unaware. Like sitting ducks. No telling what they would've done, and Trey wouldn't have known until it was too late.

First couple of names that came to mind—Mikolas and Woodrow. He hoped he was wrong. Regardless, whoever was out there likely needed help, or they wouldn't be splashing, and once Trey grabbed his coiled lariat, he took off running after Zurina. She'd ignored his command to wait for him, and he caught up with her a fair ways up the bank.

She pointed into the water. "Over there. See him?"

"Who?" His glance searched for, found and fastened over a shape several yards upstream.

"He's terrified, Trey. We have to pull him out."

The unmistakable shape of a sheep. Sticking head and neck out of the water.

The alarm drained out of him. Trey set his hands on his hips in exasperation. "What the hell is he doing out there?"

"He must have gotten confused and fallen in. Will your rope reach?"

"He's just standing out there." The damn fool.

"He's not bleating, either, which means he's scared. Sheep are very vulnerable, Trey. They don't know how to defend themselves."

Vulnerable? Stupid was more like it, but Trey

knew better than to say so. And though it scraped against every grain in his cattleman body, he had to do what he could to save the woolly.

For Zurina's sake, he told himself.

Zurina's.

He adjusted the lariat's honda to make the right size loop, lifted his arm and started the circle spinning. Gauging his toss, he threw the loop, but the sheep floundered at the sight of the hemp coming at him. Floundered so much, he went right under. The lariat missed, and Zurina yelped in horror.

"Try again, Trey. Hurry, or he'll drown!"

The woolly came up bobbing and splashing. Trey swung the loop a second time. By now, the sheep was good and panicked, and the rope missed its mark. Again.

"I have to go in." Zurina lifted her sweater by its hem and yanked the garment over her head.

"The hell you will." Trey pulled the rope in and readied for another swing. He'd roped plenty of ornery cows in his day, and he'd be damned if one tongue-tied, water-logged woolly would best him, but before he could throw out his rope again, Zurina had her boots pulled off and her skirt unbuttoned.

Trey gaped at her. "Don't even think about jumping in after him, Zurina. The water's damn cold."

"It's not deep."

"You could step into a hole. As dark as it is, I'd never see you to find you."

"He's full-woolled, Trey. The water has soaked the fleece and is weighing him down. His legs aren't strong enough for him to climb out." Her skirt and blouse lay in a heap over her sweater. She perched on the edge of the bank in her thin shift.

Trey could hardly contain his annoyance. He heaved a disgusted sigh and began unbuttoning his shirt.

"I'll go in after him, then, Zurina. Stay here, and I mean it. Put your clothes back—"

She was in the water before he could finish the sentence. The cold sucked a shriek right out of her, but she kept on going, straight toward the woolly she was so determined to save.

The worthless piece of mutton. Trey bit back a curse. He would've throttled her if he could've reached her. He wavered between going in after her and hanging onto good sense and staying dry on the bank.

Good sense won out, but his eyes glued themselves to her moonlit shape. She waded in water that soon reached her waist. A few feet from the sheep, she twisted back toward Trey.

"Throw me the rope," she said and stretched out her hand.

Her teeth were chattering, and he hurried to throw the loop right to her. She grasped the line and would've draped it over the sheep's head, but he suddenly shied and knocked her sideways.

She went under with a cry, and Trey's heart forgot to beat.

Cussing the air blue, he leaped into the creek. Water seeped into his boots and socks. He reached Zurina just as she came up with a gasp.

"Oh God, it's freezing!" Arms flailing, she half-giggled, half-shrieked, and did a fast two-step to keep her balance.

Feet braced, Trey scooped her up against him and held on to her good and tight. Her toes cleared the creek bottom by inches.

"Are you all right?" he demanded.

She circled her arms around his neck. "Yes, of course. Oh, but I am so sorry!"

Her wet skin and soggy shift soaked into his shirt. Water seeped higher up his Levi's but every drop was worth it to be able to hold her like this. As if she was wearing nothing at all.

He eased her down into the water. The thin undergarment plastered her body like a second skin, and his hands slid lower, cupped her cool buttocks and pulled her harder against him.

"Sorry for what?" he murmured.

Fire flared in his groin, and from the thickening of his shaft, she would know how her near-nakedness affected him.

"For making you w-wet and c-cold," she breathed.

"Do I look mad over it?"

His head lowered, and his mouth took hers in bold and selfish thievery, taking advantage of a situation that demanded restraint, considering their predicament. Yet his hunger, his burgeoning, persistent need for her warred with his good sense. He took her mouth with long, deep strokes of his tongue, showing her just what he'd like to do to her with his body…until her soft, shivering moans reminded him where they were. And why.

Reluctantly, he lifted his head and ended the kisses. He slid his hands up and down her arms, warming her.

"Yeah, woman. You owe me," he growled, and took the rope she still held. "But first, let's get this damn fool woolly out of the water before we both catch our deaths."

"It will not be e-easy," she warned.

Trey looped the rope over the sheep's neck and soon found truer words were never spoken. Together, they pulled, tugged and pushed the sheep toward the bank. At times panicked, at others as stiff as a statue, the scared animal resisted their efforts to be rescued.

But eventually, they managed it. Once up on the bank, Trey sank to the ground. Zurina collapsed beside him, both of them exhausted from their efforts.

"We must get him away from the w-water," she panted. "Or else he—oh, no!"

Before Trey could even *think* it, the stupid sheep turned tail and jumped right back into the creek.

Chapter Thirteen

The fire shed a glorious heat that soaked into Zurina's bones and painted her skin with a rosy glow. After their efforts to rescue the panic-stricken ewe a second time, she hadn't been sure she could ever get warm again.

Trey made sure she did. He built two fires—one to dry their clothes, the other to dry themselves. He'd wrapped her in a blanket and parked her as close to the flames as he dared, then plunked a cup of steaming hot coffee into her hands with strict instructions to drink every drop.

Zurina admitted to enjoying his fussing. His worrying. Really, she could have done all those things herself—build a fire, wrap up in a blanket, pour a cup of coffee—but when Trey did them for her, well, he made her feel…special to him.

Imagine. A cattleman taking such good care of a Basque sheepwoman. Who would have thought it could happen?

And yet, she couldn't let herself enjoy it too much. This camaraderie they shared—it wouldn't last much longer. When he found out about Mikolas, the hate and resentment both Mikolas and Zurina harbored for the terrible violence Sutton Wells enacted against Mama, reality would come crashing down on their heads, and nothing would be the same again.

Zurina had tried to tell Trey earlier, before the sheep's splashing distracted her. Trey deserved to know about his half brother. He needed to know what to expect when they finally met in Rogers Pass, if indeed that's where Mikolas was, hiding out with Woodrow Baldwin.

Zurina dreaded what would happen. Mikolas had been so angry when she saw him last. So full of vengeance...

She couldn't bear to think of it. Later, she would have to. But for now, just for tonight, she preferred to think of only Trey.

Her glance settled over him while he finished pounding the last of a row of sticks into the ground, near the fire. Bare-chested, muscles rippling, his work absorbed him. Her socks already hung drying from a couple of the little posts, next to his boots. And strung between two trees, a rope held her shift and Trey's shirt.

It wouldn't be long, and he would add his soaking wet Levi's to the line, and a warmth pooled inside Zurina, deep between her thighs.

He would be completely naked, then. Just like Zurina was now, beneath the blanket, and oh, what a strange feeling it was sitting here like that. As naked as the day she was born.

Neither of them had any choice, of course. Sleeping in their wet clothes would have been cold and uncomfortable. Silly, too. The garments would dry far faster hanging by themselves during the night, close to the fiery heat.

Still, she missed the clothes she'd left behind in her room. Clean underwear, folded neatly in the drawer. Her skirts and blouses, each dry and ready to pull on.

But they were there. And she was here, a half day's ride away.

Her thoughts drifted to her sweater, skirt, blouse and boots, and how they still laid along the creek's bank. Somewhere. She'd lost track of them in the dark. After they brought the sodden ewe back to camp and hobbled her, Trey didn't want Zurina traipsing along the bank in her wet shift searching for her clothes. She would just have to go back for them in the morning.

"Warm enough?"

Trey's low voice reached into her musings and

sent them flying. He squatted next to her, his forearm propped on his knee.

"Very much so." But she clutched the blanket tighter. "How about you?"

His coppery eyes smoldered, in a way that had nothing to do with their close proximity to the flames.

"Getting warmer by the minute," he murmured.

Her bare toes curled into the grass. The way he looked at her. As if he could devour her with smacking lips and relish every bite...

He reached out a long arm and tucked her hair behind her ear. She could imagine how she looked to him, with her braid undone, her dark tresses spread over her shoulders to dry, wisps curling at her temples.

"Unless you need something, we might as well turn in," he said.

"I don't need anything," she said softly. "But thank you."

He drew back, straightened, and with her heart pounding, she watched him stride to their clothesline. He unbuttoned his pants, hooked his thumbs over the waistband and peeled the wet denims down past his thighs.

Her pulse pounded harder. Firelight accented the muscles rolling over his shoulders and lean, taut buttocks. The breadth of power in this man had never been more apparent, more breathtaking, than now.

When he was stark naked.

She quickly averted her gaze before he turned and caught her staring. She set aside her cup and busied herself adjusting her blanket, keeping herself cocooned within its folds while she changed from a sitting position to a reclining one, no easy task for sure.

But she managed, thank goodness, and before he returned. He'd made a small bed by spreading a long, rubber-backed tarp over pine needles and grass, and she shifted to her side near the very edge, facing the fire, and closed her eyes.

Yet every sense tuned into him. The rustle of denim being shook out and hung over the rope line. The faint crunch of grass from quick strides across the camp to join her here, next to the fire. She didn't need to see him to know when he halted, then knelt behind her.

"Going to have to split that blanket with me, Zurina," he said. "It's the only one we have. There's room enough for both of us, and it'll be warmer, besides."

Her eyes flew open. "You don't have another one for yourself?"

"On a pack horse I do, back with the posse. I wasn't planning on sharing my bedroll with anyone when we parted ways this afternoon. Now hurry, sweet. It's cold."

She bit her lip. Any red-blooded woman would

see herself at a distinct disadvantage under the circumstances.

Sleeping naked with Trey Wells.

"C'mon, Zurina." He tugged on one edge of her very warm, very safe cocoon.

She didn't budge. Oh God, she couldn't. She couldn't very well keep the blanket all to herself, either, but really, she *couldn't...*

One side of the cocoon jerked open, hard enough to jostle her and let in a draft of cold air against her backside. But like a window, once he settled in, the chill disappeared.

Delicious warmth returned.

Zurina kept on her side and lay very still. She expected him to touch her.

Feared it.

Wanted it.

She held her breath and waited....

The blanket rustled again. A moment passed. Zurina envisioned him propped up on his elbow, watching her.

But not touching her.

"Are you afraid of being with me like this?" he asked in his low voice.

Lifting her head, she darted him a cautious glance over her shoulder. "I'm a little nervous, yes."

"Don't be."

"It is—" she searched for the right word "—risky."

"Risky."

To her surprise, he broke into a chuckle, a deep-throated sound she'd not heard from him before, but one she found very pleasant. Considering.

"For you? Or for me?" he asked.

Her brow shot up. "For me, of course."

"Because I'm one of those cattlemen you despise so much?"

"Because I'm only a woman—"

She halted.

A woman who won't be able to resist you if you try to seduce me.

As if he read the words spilling through her mind, his amusement faded.

"I've yet to force my attentions on a woman who didn't want them, Zurina. Including you. You should know that about me by now."

He sounded offended she might've thought otherwise, and bemused, she eased onto her back.

How different he was from his father, Sutton Wells. Mama had suffered greatly from the force of his "attentions."

Yet Trey need only recall how Zurina had melted in his arms from the power of his kisses. He made her forget who he was, what his father had done, and turned her mindless of any contempt she'd ever felt for him.

Instead she'd grown to think of him—and want him—in a far different way.

As if she'd fallen in love with him.

Was it possible?

"What makes you think Mikolas will be at Rogers Pass?" Trey asked suddenly.

The inevitable confrontation with her brother laid heavily on his mind, for he asked the question in all seriousness. Perhaps he chose to distract her from her misgivings, or merely wanted to make her feel at ease with her nakedness—and his.

She allowed herself the distraction. It was far easier to talk about her brother than wrestle with her own tortuous thoughts.

"I'm not sure if he'll be there," she said quietly. "But I'm hoping, very much."

"Hell of a lot of country out here," he said. "Why the pass?"

Zurina tumbled through memories she'd long repressed. She understood Trey's need to arm himself with as much information as possible. She knew all he had at stake.

But, oh, it hurt to think of the nightmare again.

"There is something to tell you. Something no one besides my family knows," she said so softly, her voice was almost a whisper.

"Go on," he urged, his expression darkly serious. "I'll honor your confidence."

She pressed her fingers to her lips, but pulled them away again to let the words out, the explanation he wanted to hear.

"When I was twelve, Papa herded a band of sheep

not far from here. Gorri wasn't much more than a pup, but he was already a fine sheepdog. He ran after several lambs that had gotten separated from their mothers. Wanting to help, I followed him, but he was too fast for me, and I got lost."

Trey grunted in commiseration and waited for her to continue.

"A fur trapper found me. Or maybe he was an outlaw on the run. I never knew for sure. He took me to his cabin, and—and tied me to his filthy bed."

In her darkest memories, Zurina could smell his fetid breath, see his whiskey-reddened eyes, his wild, tangled hair. But mostly, she would never forget the heaviness of his groping hands on her young, maturing body ....

"God, Zurina." Trey smoothed the wisps against her temple, and she angled her face toward him, craving his strength even now, after all these years.

"It seemed like forever, but Mikolas finally found me in that tiny cabin hidden in the woods. Gorri helped, and when the man caught us trying to escape, Mikolas shot him with Papa's rifle."

The same old rifle still in its scabbard and lying within easy reach of their bedroll.

Trey studied her with his brows furrowed. Her story held him fast in the telling.

Her mouth quirked in rueful dismay. "If that weren't enough, while we were running from the cabin, trying to get back to Papa and the others, we startled a big grizzly bear. He charged, and Mikolas shot him again and again, until the bear dropped."

"Hell."

Trey looked so appalled, she couldn't help reaching out and touching his cheek. A gesture intended to reassure him. And a plea that he would understand.

"He saved my life twice that day, Trey," she said. "He's not as heartless as you think."

Trey turned his face and pressed a lingering kiss into her wrist.

"I want to believe he's a good man, for your sake," he said. "But the cold, hard truth is in that ransom note he sent us."

The feel of his lips so tender against her skin softened the harshness of his claim. Every word, he meant.

"Yes, I know," she said on a troubled sigh. Her fingertips trailed along his cheek toward the corner of his chin. And stayed there, imploring him to believe her. "He has good reasons for being with Woodrow and for keeping Allethaire. I don't know what they are, but we must trust him in that."

Trey made a sound of disgust and would've pulled away, except Zurina cupped his face with both her hands, keeping him close to her, a boldness she hardly realized in her need to keep him listening.

Trey Wells was a powerful man, bent on revenge. A man capable of protecting those he held dear, at the cost of those he didn't. The time had not yet come to tell him the truth about Mikolas. Trey wasn't ready. Not when he wore his animosity like a thorny badge.

It was more important to teach him about the good in Mikolas first. The Mikolas Zurina had always known.

"Please, Trey," she said quietly. "Do not judge him until you see for yourself the kind of man he is. Until he gives us the answers we need."

The flames cast Trey's features in a muted golden light, but the copper glints in his eyes darkened to tarnished bronze, revealing the inward battle he waged. He was silent so long, she feared she'd lost the fight.

Her thumb stroked the strong line of his chin. "Will you do this for me, Trey?"

Slowly, finally, he nodded. "Yes." His hand moved to curl behind her neck. "But only for you, Zurina."

His head lowered, and her breath hitched with instant anticipation of what he intended to do. The kisses he intended to give. He wouldn't stop at one, her womanly heart told her. Or even two, and with crystal, blood-stirring clarity, she realized she didn't want him to stop.

Maybe never, and not anymore. Because now Mikolas didn't matter. Or Woodrow. Or Allethaire. Nothing mattered but this desire, this crazy, incessant need which had been building between them.

Demanding satisfaction.

Trey's mouth captured hers with a sudden fierceness that fueled the fire in her blood. His long fingers splayed into her hair and lifted her head to keep her mouth hard against his. He kissed her long, deep, so deep she could barely breathe. Could barely think of anything but this man who'd wound his way into her heart and consumed her soul.

His tongue penetrated her lips with sure, masterful strokes. A deft seduction of her senses which turned his breathing ragged and left Zurina aching for more.

So much more.

Trey's seduction of her mouth ended with rasping kisses dragged over her cheek, her jaw, the sensitive skin along her throat and around her ear. He licked. And nibbled. He whispered her name again and again.

She was drowning. Flying. Somersaulting toward exhilaration. He tore away her inhibitions, turned her slave to his pleasure. To her own. No longer were they divided by the boundaries of cattleman and sheepwoman, but instead, simply man and woman, with a blinding, intoxicating passion for one another.

His hand found her breast, and he cupped the mound in his broad palm. Flexed and fondled, both gentle and rough, giving and taking.

The desire climbed, swelled into her veins, yet he

pulled her still higher with the exquisite rub of his thumb over her nipple.

No man had ever touched her like this, with such mastery, with such intent to give pleasure and take it, too. He pulled down the blanket with a low-throated groan and bent his head to her breast, took a nipple into his mouth with a strong, glorious suckle, and her back arched with a gasp. The sensation was almost too much to bear when he repeated his seduction on the other, yet her fingers speared into his hair, holding him to her. If only he could make her feel like this forever, but no, she would surely die. Surely die...

Moisture pooled between her legs, in her most intimate femininity, and her hips turned into him with a primitive plea to end the delicious agony.

"Zurina, my sweet," he murmured and reached between them, lifted her thigh and brought it up over his hip. She never thought to deny him what he sought, not when she wanted utter completeness with him, only him...

The hot velvet of his shaft pressed against the moist folds of her cleft, seeking his place inside her. He was prepared to take what he wanted, what they both needed, but a desire to touch him first, to discover the beauty of his masculinity, suddenly coursed through her.

Never had she known such boldness, but she knew it now. She reveled in the freedom to hold him without shame or embarrassment.

Her fingers closed around his pulsing erection, fondled and caressed and savored, and he hissed in a hard breath. God, but he was well-hung, and oh, the feel of his ballocks, turgid with a sprinkling of crisp, dark hairs—

Trey cursed and pushed her onto her back. He rose above her with his expression shadowed, but his eyes glittering from arousal.

"I'm going to take you, Zurina. I can't much stop myself. I want to crawl inside you and into your skin and become a part of you right now."

His wide shoulders carried a sheen of sweat. The blanket had slipped from them both, but she felt no chill from the night and its mountain air. No shame from their nakedness. It was right to be with him like this, on the brink of a sublime and perfect joining.

So very right.

Yet for a moment he didn't move. Just held himself above her, his breathing rough and his control precarious.

Time, she realized. He gave her time to stop him and end the loving. To save herself from what he was about to do.

How could he not know how much she wanted him? That her need ran like wildfire through her blood, just like his?

"Come into me, Trey."

Her knees fell open. Her legs lifted to curl around his waist. She slid her hands up his lean belly, over his ribs, glided onto his coin-shaped nipples, dark as coffee in the flames' light, and up to his hard-muscled shoulders. Bulging, quivering, with restraint.

"Come into me," she begged.

"Zurina," he breathed. "Zurina, Zurina."

She sensed the exact moment his honor gave way to lusty greed. He clasped her hips and lifted her into position in front of him, finding her female folds with the tip of his shaft. He thrust into her slickness, and she gasped at the sensation, at how her soft, tight flesh opened to accommodate him.

Oh God, he filled her. Filled her so full, so deep, she feared he'd wrench her apart.

But a sweeter agony she'd never known. A sweeter ecstasy she'd never craved.

Her breathing turned into ragged little gasps; he thrust again and then again, finding his place inside her, claiming her with a fierce possessiveness she would forever hold, deep in her heart.

Like a coil, white-hot from the fire, the tension built inside her with his every thrust. Built and built, until she could go no higher, until the coil snapped, and she fell into a river of glorious, mind-spinning sensation.

Trey threw back his head with a guttural roar. With one final, earth-shattering thrust, he spilled his seed inside her. And afterward, in slow motion, completely spent, he collapsed on top of her.

Chapter Fourteen

"Tell that damn woolly to shut up, Zurina."

Trey's mumble dragged her out of the depths of luscious slumber. His breathing stirred her hair, and his big body molded to her backside. Like they were a pair of spoons in a silverware chest.

Persistent bleating intruded into her languor, and then, Zurina understood. Her mouth softened. She supposed Trey was entitled to complain. He was a cattleman, after all.

"She's telling us she's happy this morning," Zurina murmured patiently, not bothering to open her eyes. "She feels safe and isn't afraid like she was last night."

The fire crackled and spit and shed a blanket of heat around them, which meant Trey had gotten up not long ago, added more wood and stirred the embers. She didn't have to open her eyes to know the sun had crept over the horizon, either. Or envision how she laid in Trey's arms, with his fist relaxed near her chin.

She didn't want to wake up at all. She wanted to lie like this forever.

"Are *you* happy, Zurina?" he asked, his tone husky.

He nuzzled her hair, cupped her breast and helped himself to a leisurely fondle, reminding her of how they'd made love again last night, and how well he'd come to know her body.

Like a husband.

Every intimate inch.

Sighing her contentment, she rolled over to face him and slid her arms around his neck. She marveled at how familiar she'd become with him. How easy it was to snuggle up to him like this.

"Very," she admitted.

He emitted a male-cat growl, clearly satisfied with her response and taking full responsibility for it. He pressed a hand to the small of her back and pulled her even closer, then took her mouth for a long, languid kiss. The thickening of his shaft against her thigh proved fair warning his ardor was gathering steam again, and she would soon feel the heat of it.

But unexpectedly, he ended the kiss and eased back.

"I can hardly think with all that noise she's making," he muttered.

"So don't think. Only feel."

Zurina tugged him down to kiss her again. She drew his lower lip between her teeth and nibbled, took her time in tracing his upper lip with her tongue, and engaged him in some playful and very wet, very arousing, mouth games—until even she had to admit the ewe's constant *baa-ing* was an unwelcome distraction.

Zurina drew away with a frustrated pout. "Maybe she doesn't want to be hobbled anymore."

"Damned if I know what her problem is." His scowl showed him just as frustrated. "You're the sheep expert. Not me."

Zurina sighed and smoothed the hair from his forehead. She loved the feel of his hair, thick and cool and soft.

"I'm sorry," she said, feeling almost guilty for rescuing the poor woolly from the creek. "We should let her go."

"Good idea."

Yet he didn't move. They both knew when he did, a change would creep between them, stealthy and sure. Like a gossamer veil, hiding all they shared during the night, but not quite taking it away.

They had so little time left to meet the terms of the ransom note. Only hours to get dressed and ride up to Rogers Pass. If Mikolas wasn't there with Woodrow and Allethaire, well, it'd be a fast ride down again to rendezvous at Wolf Creek.

Then, all hell would break loose.

The ugliness would begin.

How she wished she could turn back time and relive all the glorious moments with Trey again! Shut out the world with its secrets and betrayals and make love with him again and again. *Live* love with him. For the rest of their lives.

She couldn't, of course. And she was a fool to let her foolish longings deter her from the reality of what laid ahead.

Trey flung back his side of the blanket. "It's late. I'll brew up some coffee and help you find the clothes you left on the bank."

He tucked the wool covering closer around her, rose and swiftly strode on the balls of his feet over the dew-damp grass, grabbing his socks and boots on the way to the rope line. Her gaze clung to his tall, muscular body in all its naked, masculine magnificence.

The evidence of his arousal in particular.

Why did she have to fall in love with him? When he learned the truth, he'd despise her for her cowardliness in not telling him sooner. He'd think she was deceiving him for her brother's sake, and oh God, what did it matter anymore?

He could never be hers.

Levi's and boots on, his shirt not yet buttoned,

Trey squatted in front of her, holding her white cotton shift and thick socks.

"All dry and still warm," he said with a disarming smile.

Unexpected tears stung her eyes. These little ways he took care of her—she had to garner all her will to fight the emotion down. She couldn't let his thoughtfulness keep her from what she had to do.

She sat up, letting the blanket slide off her while she pulled the toasty warm undergarment over her head. Once through the neckline, she encountered Trey's stare, stark from simmering passion, on her uncovered breasts.

Her nipples quickly pebbled, whether from the chilly morning air or the heat of his gaze, she couldn't be sure, but moments ago, she would've succumbed to another round of lovemaking while Trey took it upon himself to warm her up good and right.

But now, he had to know about his brother. Zurina had delayed long enough.

She tugged the shift down. "I have something to tell you, Trey."

His gaze lifted to meet hers, and he started fastening his shirt.

"I'm listening," he said.

"It's about Mikolas."

"What about him?"

She pulled on her socks with unsteady fingers. She'd feel better being dressed, even with what little clothing she had. Less vulnerable. She stood, and her shift drifted over her thighs. Trey stood with her.

She took a breath. "He's your brother."

Trey kept buttoning, one after the other, but the movements had turned savage.

"What game are you playing with me, Zurina?"

She shivered at the lethal undertones in his voice. "It's the truth."

"You're lying."

"My mother told us, just before she died."

"She was lying to you, then."

"Your father *raped* her, Trey. Mikolas was the result of—of that."

He went still. So still his silence terrified her. She didn't dare move, didn't dare speak. The blood pounded in her veins.

Then, a dangerous calm appeared to come over him, like sun through thundering clouds. He finished the last button and stuffed the shirttails inside the waistband of his Levi's.

"Have you ever met my father?" he asked.

"No." After what he'd done to her mother all those years ago, she was glad she never would.

"And yet you believe he was capable of forcing himself on a woman," Trey said.

"I believe it because that woman told me so."

"Your father, Gabirel, never indicated to me—"

"My father is a fair man, Trey. He never held you accountable for your father's sin." Which had been committed when Trey was very young and several years before Zurina had been born. If Papa had attempted any retaliation against Sutton Wells, he never told her so, even after Mama died. "It was more important to think of the sheep."

His lip curled. "The sheep."

Her father would do everything he could to keep from jeopardizing Sun River Valley and his agreement with Trey to use the plentiful grass there. Until Zurina had convinced Papa to leave, that is.

"Guess now that he's dead, the Wells Cattle Company is ripe pickin's," Trey drawled. "Isn't it, Zurina?"

The accusation burned right through her.

"No," she said and recalled the ominous ransom note. "I mean, yes, but—"

"Never thought you'd prostitute yourself for my money, sweetheart," he said smoothly. "Guess that makes you no better than Mikolas and sitting on the same wagon as Woodrow."

She sucked in a breath and bled from his hostility. How could he accuse her of conspiring with the man who'd massacred her sheep? How could he think she'd be that devious? That stupid? Because she was Basque and therefore not capable of respectability? Morals and honor? *Intelligence?*

Of course, that's what he thought. He was a cattleman, and he may as well have reached out and slashed her with a knife for the pain he inflicted.

"Don't you dare compare me to him," she said hoarsely, blinking fast.

"Just calling a spade a spade, sweetheart."

"Damn you, Trey. What happened between us last night had nothing to do with Woodrow or Mikolas," she said.

Why didn't he realize she gave him what she'd never given a man before—and a cattleman to boot? That no Basque woman would've shamed herself by sinking so low, and yet Zurina had done just that?

"You wouldn't be the first woman to use her body to get what she wants." A muscle ticked in his jaw. "And I wouldn't be the first man to fall for it."

"I'm getting my clothes."

Zurina refused to hear any more. Deep down, she knew he was hurting from what his father had done, just like Mikolas hurt. Disbelief, contempt, lashing out against those nearest to them...she understood.

But she was hurting, too. Just like they were. Trey was too blind, too full of contempt, to see it, or much care.

Zurina pivoted and headed for the creek's bank. He let her go, and she kept going, her stockinged feet moving faster the farther away she got, yet her ears strained to hear his boot steps behind her. She ached to hear him call her name, to give them a chance to start over again.

To make their lives as wondrous as they'd been last night.

He didn't come, though, and she broke into a run. Her skin turned numb to the morning chill, her cheeks oblivious to their wetness. She feared what Trey would do next, how he would fight Mikolas. If blood would spill…

Mikolas would be no match for a man of Trey's power, and Woodrow, oh God, Woodrow. The man she hated most of all. A man who slaughtered innocent sheep, and he would stop at nothing to hurt Trey if Trey didn't meet his demands.

And Trey wouldn't.

But then, what of Allethaire?

Misery washed over Zurina, heavy and thick and suffocating. Dear God, how would this all end? Who would suffer? Who could possibly win?

Absorbed with heartache, she almost missed her clothes strewn along the bank, right where she'd dropped them, and she fell to her knees, covered her face with her hands and prayed. Prayed for strength to find Mikolas. To fight Woodrow. To help Allethaire.

But mostly, she prayed for herself. For strength to go on without Trey, when he despised her so much, and she loved him.

She loved him.

Slowly composure returned. Or at least, a mellowing of her fears. She'd never be able to hunt down that old cabin in Rogers Pass if her mind was twisted up in knots, and she swallowed down her despair.

Scrubbed her cheeks dry. Put on her blouse and skirt and topped them off with her sweater.

Somehow, being fully dressed again bolstered her resolve. Only her boots remained; she sat and pulled on one boot and reached for the second.

Her glance snagged on a set of prints in the mud.

Each large, with five toes and five claw indentations. And as far as she could tell, fairly recent.

Bear tracks. Her glance lighted on a large pile of dung nearby, still glistening—

He was somewhere close, and the tiny hairs rose on the back of her neck. He must have come to the creek to forage for fish, or maybe only a drink, but all of a sudden, she was twelve again. Mikolas had just shot the wild-haired fur trapper, and they were escaping, just as the giant grizzly came at them, charging with his sharp teeth bared, his mammoth paws reaching, reaching—

A low, rumbling growl floated toward her and prickled against her nerve endings. Her gaze shot in the direction of the sound, and there he was, a short distance into the trees, bent over a carcass of something she couldn't determine. If he noticed her, he would see her as a threat to his food. He would strike out to protect his kill, and the urge to run surged through her, so strong she shook from the onslaught.

Yet she forced herself to put on her boot. To stay

calm. If she could slip away unnoticed, she'd run better, faster, with both feet shod.

Her fingers shaking, she managed and stood. Her heart pounded so hard, she could barely breathe. She took one step back, then another, but a third clipped a protruding tree root. She grappled for balance but failed, and she went down with a startled squeak.

The grizzly caught the sudden movement of her fall, and his big head swung around. His fierce black eyes fastened over her, a new prospect for prey, and he straightened on his hind legs.

Sunlight dappled through the leaves and pine branches and turned the tips of his deep red pelt silver. He stood like a monster, at least seven feet, maybe eight, hundreds of pounds, maybe even a full *thousand*, and if he charged toward her, if he tried to maul her, she'd be powerless, powerless—

"Roll over, Zurina, and do it now."

Her horror cracked at the sound of Trey's terse voice in the shadows of a willow tree. He stood with his Winchester rifle to his shoulder, the barrel leveled at the bear's heart. She nearly wept with relief.

"I've got you covered, Zurina. Do what I tell you."

She obeyed when every cell in her body cried out to jump up and run toward him. It was one of the hardest things she'd ever had to do—take her eyes off that grizzly and lay her life in Trey's hands.

But she did and pressed her cheek into the damp grass.

"Spread your feet and hide your hands," he ordered slowly. "And whatever the hell you do, don't look at him."

Zurina swallowed hard. *Play dead. Appear defenseless. Make myself hard to flip over, yes, yes, yes...*

She squeezed her eyes shut and repeated the mantra, assuring herself to lay still would save her life—and so would Trey.

Yet the faint thud reverberating through the earth beneath her cheek incited a new wave of terror. The bear had begun a lumbering walk toward her, and what if he saw through her ruse and knew she wasn't dead at all? What if he kept coming and scooped her up with his mammoth, sharp-as-a-switchblade claws?

A gunshot barked through the silence, and Zurina nearly jumped out of her skin. Bits of dirt and fallen pine needles pelted her, and the bear roared, a harrowing sound that pushed a scream into her throat.

Trey fired into the ground again. And again. Her eyes flew open to see for herself what the grizzly was doing—he'd retreated, scared away by the gunfire, and oh, sweet Jesus, sweet Jesus.

Zurina shuddered in supreme relief and pressed a fist to her mouth. The toe of Trey's boot appeared in front of her, and he hunkered down.

"He's gone," he said. "Let's go."

Clasping her elbow, he helped her to her feet and would have hustled her back to camp, but she pulled free and stole precious time to peer up at him.

He made no move to take her into his arms and give the comfort she craved. Not so long ago, he would have, in no uncertain terms, with his body and his kisses.

"Thank you," she said, the words unsteady. "I don't know what I would've done if you hadn't come."

His sharp gaze raked over her, as if to assure himself she wasn't hurt. "I shouldn't have let you come out here by yourself."

"You couldn't have known he'd be out here."

"I should have."

"Trey."

She ached to touch him, feel his hard, strong body against her. He blamed himself for what had almost happened, and if only she could take back all she told him about Mikolas and make things right between them again. She'd wrap her arms around him and kiss him until all their guilt melted away...

But that would only mean she was—what was the word he used?—prostituting herself again.

So she didn't.

"Never mind," she said.

If he had an inkling of what she was about to do,

or say, his hooded expression kept from revealing it.

"Let's go, then," he ordered, gruffly.

Again, he clasped her elbow with a firm grip, as if he refused to let her out of his sight again. He kept her moving at a fast pace back to camp. Along the way, his scrutiny clawed the trees around them, up and down the mountain. He kept the rifle ready under his arm, in case the grizzly reappeared.

They returned to camp unscathed. Trey had already set the ewe free, she noticed. To keep her hobbled would've made her an easy mark for a wolf. Zurina hoped she'd find her way down the mountain safely, perhaps find another sheepman's flock to join. And as full-woolled as she was, to stay out of the water.

"Collect your things," Trey commanded. "I'm ready to break camp."

Indeed, most of it was done, and her gaze lingered over the matted spot in the grass, near the banked fires. The place where she'd lain with him, shared with him tenderness and pleasure, and never would she forget her time here, on the mountain.

She tucked aside the memory and found the few supplies she'd brought with her, lying near where Trey had strung the rope line. Bending, she retied the corners of the towel. Just as she was about to join Trey, she noticed the lone red rose lying in the grass.

The one he had plucked off of Mama's bush. The one he intended to give Allethaire. It had fallen from the pocket when he hung his shirt to dry.

Carefully Zurina lifted the flower, now crushed and wilted. A single petal broke away and drifted to the ground.

It struck her, that petal. A symbol of how crushed her life had become, her dreams wilted. A symbol of Trey's, too, his life broken from all he'd learned from Zurina.

Still, perhaps Allethaire would appreciate his gesture. She wouldn't think of it as Zurina did, and Zurina tucked the flower inside the waistband of her skirt. She would return it to him later, when the time was right. When his sensibilities weren't so raw.

Waiting, he held the reins to her old mare. After she stuffed her supplies in the saddlebag, she climbed up and settled in.

Trey mounted, too, and gathered the reins into his fist.

"How old is Mikolas?" he asked roughly.

"Twenty-five."

With a slight flare of his nostrils, he slid a pensive stare over the horizon. Zurina imagined his mind working, digesting the information.

"My mother would've already died," he said, as if to himself.

Zurina didn't think there was anything proper she could say in response.

But she knew Trey would ride into Rogers Pass with what his father had done heavy on his mind.

Chapter Fifteen

The bitch couldn't cook worth crap.

Woodrow glowered down at his plate with fierce distaste. Congealed beans. Chunks of beef still raw. Half-cooked potatoes. Gravy as thin and pale as water. Never mind a lick of seasoning, and those damn biscuits, dry as shoe leather and black as charcoal, and *damn her*.

He flung the plate in a fit of rage.

Allethaire flinched from the clattering tin, but only rolled her eyes and turned her back while she dropped more of her rotten biscuits into the skillet.

Woodrow was convinced she only cooked this terrible to spite him. She didn't care how hungry he was. Or if he ate or not. She didn't care about anything but herself.

Just like all rich people.

Including the old man. And big brother, Trey.

His black kitty jumped off his lap to investigate the overturned plate, but Woodrow scooped her back up before she could. He didn't want his kitty getting sick from the rich bitch's lousy cooking.

He petted the furry back and tried not to think of his little kitty getting sick. Mama had gotten sick, and then she died....

His petting quickened. He wasn't going to let his sweet little kitty die. Not like he let Mama die. No, not his sweet little kitty, his sweet little kitty.

"Shame to waste food like that." Mikolas broke off a piece of hard biscuit and leveled him with a condescending glare. Crumbs fell into that thin gravy swimming on his plate.

"It's *crap*, not food."

Mikolas stuffed the biscuit in his mouth and took a swig of coffee that reminded Woodrow of slimy mud.

"It's a waste," he said,

Woodrow clenched his teeth against Mikolas's arguing. He'd gotten real tired of his brother's arguing lately. Real tired.

Woodrow consoled himself with the knowledge that after today, this dinner, Allethaire would never cook for him again.

"What time is it, Reggie?" he demanded.

The cowboy pulled out his shiny gold watch, stolen

off some fat banker during Reggie's last stagecoach
heist outside of Denver a couple of years ago.

Someday, Woodrow was going to have a watch
that nice. A whole drawer full, if he wanted.

"Near noon." Reggie snapped the case shut, put the
watch in his pocket and went back to his dinner.

"Couple more hours, then we'll clear out," Woodrow said.

He could hardly wait to go. A short trip out of the
pass, then on to Wolf Creek to wait for Big Brother,
then this whole thing would be over.

Woodrow knew just the spot to hide, too, where
he'd be able to see if Trey came by himself, or if he'd
try to sneak in with the law.

Woodrow was no fool when it came to his big
brother. He knew he had to be ready for anything
Trey might try to pull.

"He's never going to give you that money, you
know," Allethaire said.

Woodrow's eyes slitted over her. Smoke curled
from the skillet, fair warning she was on her way to
burning another batch of biscuits.

"Shut up," he said.

Her mouth wasn't as swollen today, and he reck-
oned that was a good thing. He couldn't give her over
to Trey as damaged goods, could he? Though he'd
been tempted to hit her again plenty of times since,
he'd managed to restrain himself.

Woodrow prided himself on it. God, he detested

a high-handed woman. One who couldn't cook even more.

"It's true," Mikolas said. "He won't."

Woodrow swung his gaze. "You shut the hell up, too, Mikolas."

Ever since Mikolas found out about what Woodrow had done to his family's sheep, Mikolas had turned tail on him. Woodrow could feel it, though Mikolas hadn't said a word to indicate he had. He appeared to go along with the ransom scheme, same as always, but something was different.

Different.

Woodrow figured Mikolas didn't much trust him anymore, and the feeling was mutual. Damned shame, too, since they got along like two peas in a pod at the beginning.

So Woodrow had to change his plans a bit.

Once they got the money from Trey, and once Woodrow hired himself a good lawyer, he'd have to kill Mikolas off. That simple, and no other way around it.

Besides, getting rid of Mikolas only made Woodrow's share of the WCC bigger, and that was more important.

He was entitled. He'd known he was a Wells bastard a lot longer than Mikolas did. Years' worth of long. From what he'd been denied, he deserved as much as he could get.

Smoke curled good and thick from the skillet.

Allethaire coughed and kept waving her hand, like a stupid flag. As if all that waving was going to make them biscuits any better.

"Get the pan off the fire, woman. You're stinkin' up the camp," he yelled.

Mikolas tossed her his gloves. "Put the skillet over by the cabin. Don't burn yourself."

"No, put it over by the *trees*," Woodrow said. He was the leader, not Mikolas, and by God, he'd see to it she did things his way. "Hurry it up, too."

She took Mikolas's old gloves and pulled them on. "I should just dump them on your stupid head, Woodrow."

He stiffened at the way she spoke to him, in front of Mikolas and Reggie, especially. Who did she think she was, threatening him like that?

His fist itched to backhand her again. He had to settle for glaring at her good and mean. Ignoring him, she gripped the cast iron handle with both hands and marched to the edge of their clearing, like he told her to do. All three of them kept their eyes on her, just in case she took a notion to run off.

She didn't. Just dropped the pan in the dirt, turned around and came back with her snooty nose in the air.

"You'll see I'm right," she sniffed.

Woodrow regretted her being out of brandy. He liked her better drunk, sniveling and meek. Stone sober, she had way too much sass.

She meant Trey not giving him the ransom money, of course. Well, Woodrow had a plan of his own if Trey didn't.

"You'd better hope he has it in his hot little paw down there by Wolf Creek, honey," he said. "Or else he's going to be witness to me pumping your sorry ass full of lead and enjoying every shot."

Fear flickered over her dirt-streaked face, and the starch went right out of her. He gloated in triumph. She needed reminding who was in charge and who wasn't. If she didn't know by now he meant every word, well, she was more stupid than he thought.

After a moment, they all went back to their eating.

Everyone but Woodrow.

He settled back, cuddled with his kitty and fantasized about fine whiskey and thick, juicy steaks, compliments of his big brother and the Wells Cattle Company.

Trey was so deep in his ruminating, he'd lost track of how far they'd come.

He'd never been to this part of Bear Tooth Mountain before. He had to trust Zurina to get them to Rogers Pass and soon, so he could give Woodrow a big surprise before he headed down to Wolf Creek with Mikolas and Allethaire.

Providing they were hiding out at the pass, that is.

Earlier this morning, after leaving their camp,

Zurina had gotten her sense of direction skewed, and they were forced to retrace their steps and start over. Considering time was tight, she regretted her mistake and apologized plenty for it, but he couldn't hold the delay against her. It'd been a long time since she'd been out this way. She'd been a young girl, besides.

Mostly, he figured she had a lot on her mind. Same as he did. Last night, and all that sweet loving they'd made together, only a part of it.

Still, the suspicious side of him warned the time she'd spent with him was only a ruse. A setup, maybe. A cruel game to occupy and distract him while Mikolas and Woodrow used Allethaire to plot up some way to hit at him and the WCC.

Trey never saw Zurina's claim about Mikolas coming. He'd been stunned to hear his father could be capable of forcing himself on a woman. How could Trey have not known? Why would his father deny Trey his own flesh and blood?

Trey couldn't fathom it. Sure, Sutton Wells could be a tough son of a bitch when he had to be. He would never have built his ranch into the operation it was if he hadn't been. But he was fair, and he was honest. As far as Trey knew, his father had always respected the weaker sex and never once had Trey doubted being loved by him.

Why wouldn't Sutton love Mikolas the same way? Because his mother had been Basque? Of the sheep-herder's world?

Again and again, Trey searched for a sign that Zurina lied to him. Again and again, he failed.

Eventually logic cracked the walls of his suspicions and brought them tumbling. She believed Woodrow slaughtered her sheep. She was witness to Allethaire's kidnapping. So why would Zurina gang up with Woodrow against Trey?

But then, why would Mikolas?

Nothing made sense, yet Zurina had been genuinely horrified at seeing the ransom note. Trey had seen her horror himself. She'd been surprised when her godson, Ander, told of how he'd gotten it, too, and she'd been determined to hunt for Mikolas afterward, with or without Trey.

Trey's logic insisted if she'd been intent on deceiving him, then she'd be deceiving her father at the same time—and everyone else in her family.

If there was one thing Trey knew, Zurina would never hurt those who mattered most to her. She wouldn't hurt *anyone*, including him. There wasn't a vindictive bone in that gorgeous body of hers, only sensitivity and compassion and a capability to love that left him awed and hungering.

Hell. Now that he took off his blinders and shook off his self-pity, he realized she was as much of a victim as he was. Add in the loss of her sheep—*more*.

God, he'd been such an ass.

His stomach clenched with regret for the accusations he'd hurled. His mind groped for a way to tell her so and beg forgiveness. To give him another chance.

He failed at that, too, and having no idea how to redeem himself, he swiveled a somber glance toward her.

His glance lingered.

She was so damned beautiful.

The exquisite shape of her face would be forever imprinted into his memory. The high cut of her cheekbones, her proud nose, the full bow shape to her lips...

Those warm, kissable lips.

No matter what happened up at the pass, he would always remember how she looked in the glow from a campfire, lying naked beneath him, the sheen of her skin golden. Or how she looked now, against the backdrop of pines thick on the mountains, her back straight while she sat the saddle with an easy grace. The cool air had a kick to it and feathered her cheeks with a tint of pink. She wore her hair banded at her nape, and he would never forget the feel of those long, sable tresses, either. Sliding loose and slow through his fingers. Or pooled in a silken heap on his shoulders and chest.

Damned if he wasn't thinking like a lovesick calf, but he didn't know how he was going to leave her when everything was said and done. Or even if he should.

Before he could open his mouth and fumble his way through an apology, she abruptly sat a little straighter in the saddle.

"Look, Trey." Her dark eyes sharpened under her flat-brimmed hat. "Over there."

His sluggish brain zeroed in on smoke curling through the pines, and his thoughts cleared in a hurry. "You think it's the hideout?"

"I'm almost sure."

Most anyone could be up there, he knew. A tribe of Crow, Lakota or Cheyenne. A fur trapper or miner. Or maybe some farmer, scratching out a living in unfriendly dirt.

"It has to be," she said, almost to herself.

"Let's go up and take a look."

She tossed him a hesitant glance. "If I'm wrong, we'll never make it down to Wolf Creek in time to meet Woodrow."

"I know."

Trey debated the merits of playing it safe—complying with the terms of the ransom note—or making his own rules and going for a good dose of surprise.

He opted for surprise.

"We'll take the chance," he said.

Her quick nod told him she agreed with the decision. "All right."

"Stay beside me. Don't fall back," he ordered and nudged his horse forward, deeper into the trees.

Hers fell into step, and his senses sharpened the higher they climbed. His awareness divided between making sure Zurina kept close to him and scouring the mountain around them.

The terrain turned rougher, the pines denser. The shadows could hide a man, the tangled forest his horse. Insects buzzed; birds twittered. Twigs, fallen leaves and needles crunched beneath their mounts' hooves, and the fragrant scent of pine and damp earth filled his nostrils.

"Hoo hoodoo hooo hoo."

The bird call penetrated the multitude of forest sounds assailing his senses. Until his senses latched onto a single realization.

"Did you hear that?" he asked.

"Yes." Zurina's voice sounded hushed in deference to his. "A horned owl."

"That's right. And owls don't call during the middle of the day." He pulled his rifle from the scabbard. His muscles coiled. "They've spotted us."

"Oh, no." Alarm threaded her whisper.

"Get out your father's gun and shoot at anything that moves."

"I will not." But she pulled the rifle out and tucked the butt under her arm. "My brother is up there." She darted a quick look at him. "And so is yours."

Trey scowled, but now wasn't the time to resurrect the problem of Mikolas's parentage. "We're not going to be welcome, Zurina. If Mikolas shoots, shoot back."

"He won't shoot us. He's not a murderer."

Trey clamped his mouth shut against her loyalty. Granted, she knew the man better than he did, but Mikolas's partnering with Woodrow canceled out any allegiance Trey might've felt compelled to make.

They kept riding, one step at a time. Careful through the trees. Higher up the mountain. Closer to the scent of smoke.

Trey fought down the adrenaline itching to spill into his veins and hung on tight to control. He'd give his right arm to have Zurina safe at home with her father, but she'd been the one to get them here, and now he couldn't send her back.

Thwap!

Jesus.

A bullet hit the ground in front of them and sprayed dirt. Startled, his horse reared. Zurina cried out.

Three armed riders took shape through a stand of junipers. And kept coming. The shot warned of their presence, that any attempt to flee, or take cover, would be futile.

Trey didn't recognize any of them, but the one on the left had the look of a Basque about him.

"Are you all right, Zurina?" Trey kept his voice low, his finger ready on the Winchester's trigger.

"Yes," she said, visibly shaken.

"Is that Mikolas with 'em?"

"Yes," she said again, miserable.

His brother, and it felt damned strange to see him. Trey cursed the shadows and the man's flat-brimmed hat, which hid much of the face Trey wanted to learn.

"Know any of the others?" he demanded, pulling his scrutiny toward the pair with Mikolas.

"The one in the middle—" she paused, studying him, as if to make sure "—he took Allethaire. The man on the right, I'm not sure. He may have been the one killing most of the sheep. It was dark."

Trey's instincts suggested the man acted as accomplice on orders from Woodrow and likely posed less of a threat on his own. Which reinforced Trey's guess Woodrow would be the unquestioned leader of the gang.

And it was Woodrow who he caught eyeing him with a cold brand of glee.

"Well, well, well. If it ain't the almighty Trey Wells."

"Where's Allethaire?" Trey demanded.

"She's around."

"There's a posse nearby who won't appreciate finding her hurt, and they'll be real happy to hold you responsible," he snapped. His rifle slid over the other two. "All of you."

"You threatening us, Mr. Wells?" Woodrow taunted.

"Just telling you the way it is."

"He's right, Mikolas." Zurina appealed to her brother. "What you're doing is wrong. It's not too late to change your mind."

Mikolas's jaw hardened. "I never expected to see you riding with Trey Wells, Zurina."

His tone was frosty, but the way he kept his sights on her, Trey guessed he was more worried than mad.

"I could say the same about you and *him*." She shot an appalled glance in Woodrow's direction. "Oh, Mikolas, do you know what he's done?"

"I know," he said.

Pain flickered across his expression, and Trey realized Mikolas wasn't as unaffected by the sheep his family had lost as he liked everyone to think.

"Then how can—"

"That's enough of your jawin', woman." Woodrow barked the order with a jerk of his Colt's barrel. "Put down your rifles, both of you."

"Don't talk to her like that, Woodrow," Mikolas said, not moving. "You've hurt her enough."

"Make her do like she's told, then, and she won't be hurt anymore."

"I'm warning you, Woodrow. She's not the one we've got a grievance against."

Woodrow glared at him, then heaved a long-suffering sigh. "Listen up, Mikolas. We don't have time for female theatrics, all right? We've got business to settle, and we can't do it if we have to sit here and listen to her whine. We've got a *posse* breathing down our necks."

They engaged in a momentary battle of wills. Seemed when it came to his sister, Mikolas had a protective streak in him. Trey hadn't expected it, considering. Tension hung in the air, thick as river mud.

In the end, Mikolas backed down with a terse nod. He jerked his chin toward Zurina.

"Do as he says," he commanded.

She huffed her exasperation. "Mikolas, why are you listening to him?"

"Because he's right, damn it! Now drop your rifle."

"Fine." She tossed the old Henry to the ground in barely restrained temper.

Woodrow's gaze jumped to Trey. "Guess you're going to have to swallow your cattleman pride and drop yours, too. Unless you want us to shoot you dead right here and think of all that WCC money that you plumb won't need anymore."

He grinned with a smirk that Trey itched to remove with a well-aimed punch. But he'd come too far to risk his chances of rescuing Allethaire. He couldn't risk Zurina getting hurt, either. He wasn't yet sure how well he could protect her—or how much good Mikolas would be in defending her.

So Trey let loose with his rifle easy enough, and it landed next to hers.

"Put your hands up, nice and high, and keep 'em there," Woodrow added.

He did that, too. Zurina complied, though Trey could feel her unease building.

"Reggie, go get their guns and hand them to me. Then take their reins and lead them back to camp. Mikolas and I will ride right behind and make sure they behave themselves."

After Reggie obeyed, they pulled out. Being unarmed and captive of desperate men made for a precarious predicament. Trey kept his senses strung tight, but he figured he had a couple of things going for him that would keep him alive.

Woodrow and his gang had gone through a hell of a lot of trouble to get their hands on WCC money. They were smart enough to know they wouldn't get a dime if he was dead. Too soon to tell how Trey would keep them from succeeding, but he figured he had a fighting chance.

And that chance centered over the Basque riding behind him.

His half brother.

Might be Woodrow didn't know it yet, but there was mutiny brewing inside Mikolas, and Trey hoped he could use it to his advantage—and Zurina's.

Chapter Sixteen

Seeing the tiny cabin again brought the horror rushing back.

Zurina broke out in a cold sweat. She'd always hoped she'd never have to live that part of her past again, except here she was, a different kind of captive, this time by Woodrow Baldwin and her own troubled brother.

She yanked her glance from the horrid structure and found Allethaire nearby, roped to a tree trunk like a forgotten mongrel. That Mikolas could be at least partially to blame for the poor woman's ordeal appalled her. Who knew better than he what Zurina had gone through with that contemptible fur trapper?

Compassion welled through her at how haggard and dirty Allethaire appeared. Her hair was mussed and dull, and her dusty black dress looked as if it'd never be wearable again. But at least her eyes were no longer reddened and glazed from drink. She watched Trey and Zurina ride into camp, revolvers leveled at their backs, with alarmed surprise on her face.

"Trey!" she gasped.

His glance latched onto her. "Did they hurt you, Allethaire?"

"Yes, of course they did, but not so much that I won't see them rot in hell for it." She strained at the bindings on her wrists and around her waist, and Zurina took comfort in that she still had plenty of fight left in her. "Get me out of here. I want to go home."

"You're not going anywhere yet," Woodrow snapped. He jabbed his weapon toward Trey and Zurina. "Now get down, you two. Stand over there where I can keep an eye on you."

Unease crawled through Zurina. She'd seen for herself the cruelties he was capable of. Dismounting would leave them defenseless and robbed of any means of escape.

"Do as he says, Zurina."

Trey's low voice urged her to obey, telling her they had no other choice. She detested being so vulnerable, but she climbed down, and he did the same.

The man named Reggie led their horses away. Woodrow and Mikolas dismounted, too, and stood in front of them with feet spread and Colts ready.

Immeasurable hurt spread through Zurina from her brother's betrayal, that he refused to meet her eyes when all she longed to do was run to him in relief and happiness that she'd finally found him, and he was all right. He was like a stranger to her now. No better than an outlaw, and she thanked God Papa couldn't see him like this.

Unexpectedly something inside Woodrow's shirt moved. His hand slid between the buttons and pulled out a black kitten, mewling for attention. Woodrow dropped a kiss to the little head and cuddled the feline against him.

"Well, now, isn't this a nice family reunion?" His mouth twisted in a mocking smirk. "Too bad the old man can't be with us. Isn't that right, Mikolas?"

Mikolas kept silent, but his sullen gaze riveted over Trey, who was staring right back at him. Like bulls, those two. Sizing each other up. Resisting the notion of their relation.

Suddenly Woodrow smacked Mikolas on the shoulder with the butt of his revolver.

"I said 'isn't that right, Mikolas?'" he snarled.

Mikolas swung toward him with his teeth bared.

"Don't hit me again," he yelled.

"Then answer me," Woodrow yelled back.

Mikolas's chest heaved. "I couldn't care less about Sutton Wells, y'hear? He didn't care shit about me, and he didn't care shit about you. So why should we care shit about him?"

"Because we deserve to be Wells, that's why!"

"'We'? What the hell are you talking about?" Trey demanded in a voice so low, so lethal, fear skidded down Zurina's spine. Her mind spun to understand, to believe what Woodrow insinuated....

But she had to be wrong. He couldn't have meant what she thought he said.

His revolver arced wildly at Trey. The look in his eyes turned crazy. "You're no better than us, Big Brother. Y'know that? But he loved you *more*. He loved you more, and he deserved to die 'cuz he was the worst poor-excuse-for-a-father any son could ever have."

Zurina forgot to breathe.

Trey paled.

No one moved.

The immensity of Woodrow's revelation hung in the air like a filthy cloud of smoke, robbed Zurina of thought, of speech, and held her and Trey both in the grips of disbelief.

Until the disbelief cracked wide-open, and Trey roared with a fury that rocked the mountain. He lunged for Woodrow, grabbed the front of the man's shirt with his fists and shook him hard.

"You killed him, didn't you, you stinking son of a bitch. You killed my father!"

"Get him off of me!"

Woodrow struggled against Trey's wrath while fighting to keep his hold on the kitten. Mikolas grabbed Trey, and Reggie, too, and it took both of them to peel him off Woodrow. Trey stumbled under their combined strength. The look he hurled Woodrow seethed with hate.

"I'll see you hang, I swear," he said, teeth gritted.

"Don't ever touch me again." Rage contorted Woodrow's features. He tossed the kitten aside; the little creature landed lightly on her feet and scampered off.

Woodrow stepped forward and rammed his fist into Trey's belly. Restrained, defenseless, Trey grunted from the punch and buckled, his wind lost.

Zurina screamed and bent toward him, but Woodrow grabbed her by the arm and yanked her back against his chest. He caught her unaware, forcing her to grapple for balance. He pressed the Colt's cold, hard barrel to her temple.

Woodrow trembled from a rage she suspected had been festering for years. That it was near to spilling now left her terrified of who would suffer next. Or most. She didn't dare move, didn't dare speak for fear she'd send him over the edge, and he'd pull the trigger for sure.

Breathing hard, Trey lifted his head. "Let her go, Woodrow." The bronze depths of his eyes speared venom. "You have no quarrel with her. It's me you want."

"You think I'm that stupid?" Woodrow snapped.

"She'd ride straight to the law, and don't think she won't."

"What do you want from me?" Trey demanded.

"You know what I want."

"Tell me again."

"I want my share of the WCC."

"Your share." Disdain dripped from the words.

"I'm just as much Wells as you are."

"Are you?" Trey straightened, little by little. "I don't even know *who* you are."

Woodrow cackled with cold humor. "I'm your father's bastard son, Big Brother. Just like Mikolas is. The three of us, one big, happy family."

"Family."

Trey appeared to ponder the idea. Zurina noticed his voice had lost some of its edge, but his words toyed and taunted. Slick as butter.

"That's right." Woodrow relaxed, too. But only a little. "My mother worked at Sutton's favorite saloon."

"Did she?" Trey nodded, acting interested. He stood taller. "She would've known a lot of men, then. Not just him."

Woodrow stiffened again.

"She wasn't a whore, all right? She was in love with him!" he yelled.

Trey remained unaffected. "So you want to be a real Wells, Woodrow? Like me?"

"I deserve it!"

"You know anything about driving cows? Breaking horses, that sort of thing?"

Woodrow shifted nervously. "You're trying to trick me, aren't you?"

Trey arched a brow. "Not at all."

"You're trying to make me admit I'm not as good at ranch work as you, so just give me the money, y'hear? My share of the WCC."

"Not that easy, Woodrow."

"Sure it is." The revolver's barrel lifted from Zurina's temple and gestured toward his horse. "Reggie, go fetch me a piece of paper and a pencil from my right saddlebag. Make it quick."

The moment Reggie turned to comply, Trey abruptly broke from Mikolas's grasp and barreled into Woodrow, clipping him from the side. The force jerked his weapon away from Zurina and his arm from around her shoulders.

Zurina stumbled free from his grasp, but Woodrow thought fast, and his fist came up and struck Trey's jaw. Trey's head snapped sideways, and he landed on all fours.

"Don't move, or I'll shoot!" Mikolas yelled, pointing his pistol over Trey.

Zurina's heart wrenched from the hit Trey took on her account, but it was seeing her own brother ready to kill him that hurt most of all.

She refused to stand for it, to do nothing while

Trey wavered on the brink of being killed. If Mikolas shot Trey, then he'd have to shoot her, too.

"Leave him alone, Mikolas!" She grabbed onto his arm and gave it a frantic shake.

"Stay out of this, Zurina."

Mikolas shrugged her off, but she only went for him again. "He's innocent of anything his father has done. You know he is!"

His glance jerked toward her, and for the first time, she glimpsed the agony burning in his dark eyes. His indecision. The inward battle he fought.

She knew him as well as she knew herself, and he was driven by his hurt from what Sutton Wells had done. But he'd made a mistake pairing himself with Woodrow. She sensed his realization of it. He'd gotten himself into a situation that at some point began to rage out of his control. His desperation throbbed inside him, tore at his conscience. Zurina could almost taste it in him.

And he didn't know what to do about it.

"You keep him on his knees, Mikolas," Woodrow said. "Just like you're doing, and she won't get hurt."

Once again, Zurina found herself on the wrong end of his revolver. He gripped his weapon in both hands, kept the barrel trained on her, making it clear if Mikolas didn't obey, Zurina would pay the price with her life.

Tension shimmered from Trey, like heat off

desert sand. Blood trickled from his swollen lip. He remained taut, his body coiled tight, ready to spring.

"You hurt her, Woodrow, I'll kill you," he grated. "Let her go."

"We got unfinished business, Big Brother. Nobody's going anywhere until the deal is done. Throw that paper and pencil down in front of him, Reggie, then keep your gun on him. Don't let him move. If he does, burn your powder on him," Woodrow ordered.

The man obeyed, then resumed his guarded stance, pistol leveled over Trey.

"You're going to write a little note to your banker," Woodrow went on. "You're going to tell him to draw up a draft, made out to me, Woodrow Baldwin."

"To you," Trey said.

"That's right." Woodrow's fantasy appeared to gain steam. He licked his lips. "For one half of the Wells Cattle Company."

"That much?"

"That's right. My share for being a Wells."

A share which didn't include Mikolas, Zurina realized. As if he'd forgotten Mikolas was there.

Trey knew it. Mikolas had to know it.

But her brother did nothing. Said nothing.

"Go on, Big Brother. Make sure you sign, big and clear, so he knows it was you who wrote it. And then I'll let her go."

Trey took the pencil, bent over the paper—

"Trey, don't," Zurina said, her panic rising. If the banker followed his instructions, then Trey would lose what he'd worked so hard to build with his father. Woodrow didn't deserve a dime, not one red cent for the wrongs he'd done.

But despite her plea, Trey began to write. Woodrow almost drooled in anticipation. In moments, Trey tossed him the paper.

"My final instruction," he said.

Go to hell.

For a moment, Woodrow didn't move. In the next, he threw back his head and roared with amusement.

"You want to play games with me, Big Brother? Well, I'm liking where you're at right now, y'know that?" he said, amusement fading. "On your knees in front of me. And that means you're not going to win."

"You're wasting time, Woodrow." Mikolas's patience snapped. "He's not going to give you anything. That paper says he's not."

"For your sister, he will." The grin grew bigger. "Tell me, Big Brother. Did you have a little fun with her while Allethaire was gone? Did you get under her skirts and give her a good poke now and again?"

"Shut up, Woodrow!" Mikolas yelled.

Before Trey could growl a response, Mikolas suddenly shifted his revolver's aim. Off of Trey and onto Woodrow.

Who shut up in a hurry.

His eyes narrowed to dangerous slits.

"What's wrong with you, Mikolas?" he demanded.

"Don't talk about her that way."

His eyes rounded. "What way?"

"I'm not going to let you hurt anyone anymore."

Woodrow's gaze jumped to Zurina, then back to Mikolas. "I never laid a hand on her, and if she's smart, I won't have to."

"You hurt her. You hurt my family, our sheep!"

"I didn't know they were yours, all right? I didn't know, and I said I was sorry."

"You never said you were sorry." Mikolas shook from the disgust heavy in his voice.

"I did it in my head, then," Woodrow shot back. "I *thought* I told you."

Mikolas's lip curled. "Your head."

Trey watched Mikolas close, as if to gauge the change in him. As if to determine if the change could be trusted.

"Go, Zurina," Mikolas said firmly. Unexpectedly. "Get out of here. None of this has anything to do with you."

"You don't have any business telling her what to do." Woodrow cocked the trigger. "She's just another lamb-licker, Mikolas. Just like you are, and I'm saying she's not going anywhere."

Zurina's pulse pounded. She cared little for the insults Woodrow hurled, but Mikolas stood in dangerous waters. Shoot or be shot. She didn't want to leave Trey, and she didn't want to leave Mikolas, either.

Suddenly Woodrow fired his Colt, and the sound echoed through the mountains. Mikolas spun with a yell. Blood spurted from his thigh, and he dropped to the ground.

"Mikolas!" Zurina fell to her knees beside him.

"I warned you," Woodrow spat in a cold voice. "Next time, you'll listen."

Zurina barely thought of how Woodrow could shoot her next. She fumbled with the knot on Mikolas' bandanna. "How bad are you hurt?"

"I'll live," he muttered with a grimace. The bandanna fell free, and he gripped her wrist. "I'm sorry, 'Rina."

His words, barely above a whisper, revealed his fervent regret.

"Hush." Carefully she pressed the small wad of fabric against the injury. "We'll talk later."

A furry head appeared alongside her thigh. Woodrow's kitten, curious about her ministrations. Zurina nudged her away, only to have her bound back playfully.

"Here, kitty, kitty." A woman's coaxing voice floated through the air. "Come, little kitty."

Zurina whirled. In perfect unison, everyone locked

their gazes over Allethaire strolling out of the trees. She strolled easily, as if she were enjoying the afternoon in a park.

"Come here, little kitty. Come to me," she cooed.

"What the hell?" Woodrow's head whipped toward the tree and its limp pile of rope. "How the hell—"

Allethaire extended her arm, and amazingly, the kitten frolicked toward her, a happy ball of fluff. She scooped up the creature and snuggled her under her chin. "Sweet little thing, aren't you?"

"I'm getting out of here." Reggie turned toward the horses and began to run, but suddenly a man appeared, blocking his way.

Nubby, a rifle to his shoulder.

Reggie stopped, swore and threw his hands up.

Trey's swollen mouth began to curve in stunned surprise.

Another man appeared, wearing a dark suit and a badge. Farther away, another. And another.

The camp was surrounded.

"The game's up, Woodrow," the lawman called out. "Put down your weapon."

"I want the kitty." Woodrow's eyes turned crazy. He stepped toward Allethaire. She watched him come, cool as ice. "Give her to me."

"They're going to throw you in jail, Woodrow," she said. "I don't have to do anything you tell me ever again."

"Stay right there," the police chief ordered. "Don't take a step closer to her."

"She's all I got." Woodrow shook visibly. *"Give me my kitten, you whining bitch!"*

Allethaire stood, pale, dirty, but with shoulders squared and the lawmen fanned out behind her. Woodrow pulled back the revolver's trigger, but faster, four shots rang out.

And to Zurina's unutterable horror and overwhelming relief, Woodrow Baldwin fell dead.

Chapter Seventeen

⤜⤛⤚⤙⤘⤗⤖

"Hell of a risk you took, Allethaire, setting yourself up as bait like that."

Wrapped in a blanket against the late afternoon's chill, she stood with Trey at the edge of camp while the police chief finished tying Woodrow's body onto the back of his horse.

"I was beyond caring of the risk, Trey. I only wanted him dead."

Trey could relate. The man was a sorry piece of humanity, for sure. Damned shame he claimed Wells blood in his veins.

"It was my idea, anyway." She stared at the snow-capped Bear Tooth Mountains, as if she relived the danger of what she'd done. The daring stealth of the lawmen who defied detection and set her free from the ropes that bound her was bravery at its finest.

That the police chief agreed to let her walk right back into the lion's den, well, Trey could only shake his head. If Woodrow had spotted them, if he'd had an inkling of their plan, the results would've been disastrous.

"The posse promised to cover me with all the fire-power they had. I trusted them to keep their promise," Allethaire added.

Trey let her talk. She had to get her ordeal off her chest. She'd found layers of courage inside her she didn't know she had.

"Such unforgiving country out here, isn't it?" She sounded pensive. Moody. "Hard people living hard lives. I don't know how they do it."

He declined to remind her most folks would never experience a kidnapping like she had, Zurina excepted. Nor did he speak of Montana's beauty. The crisp, clean air, grassy range as far as the eye could see, majestic mountains and rolling valleys. She should know its potential to thrive, too. Great Falls alone would one day provide enough power to bolster industry and rail transportation with its hydro-electric plant, and hell, he could talk until he was blue in the face reminding her.

She would never see Montana as he did.

Allethaire swiveled her glance back. A sad smile curved her lips. "I wasn't meant to be your wife, Trey. No matter what Daddy wanted for me. Or what we wanted for ourselves."

Slowly he nodded. "I know."

"I'm going back to Minnesota." Her expression turned rueful. "But then, you already know that, too."

"Yes." He drew in a breath, thought of all the things he should tell her. His undying love, for instance.

But he would only be lying, and that wasn't fair. To either of them.

Allethaire cocked her head and considered him. "You're smitten with her, aren't you?"

His pulse leaped. Zurina. He cleared his throat and endured a wave of guilt.

"It's very obvious, you know," Allethaire said softly.

"Is it?"

"You were terrified for her this afternoon."

"Spitless." He frowned. He would've torn Woodrow apart, limb from conniving limb, and thrown what was left of him to the wolves if he would've hurt a single hair on Zurina's head.

"Look at her," Allethaire urged.

Trey found her a score of yards away, brewing coffee for the posse over the fire, enough to fill their canteens for the long ride home. Nearby, Reggie sat hog-tied and morose. Mikolas reclined near the fire with his leg stretched out in front of him, appearing comfortable in spite of his wound.

Zurina smiled shyly at something Nubby said, and

seeing her bathed in the golden glow of the flames reminded Trey of how she looked during the glorious hours he'd made love to her.

His loins fired up, but good.

"She belongs out here, in Montana." Allethaire smiled again. "She fits."

She fit all right. The womanly curve of her hips to his. Her arms, her legs, her mouth—all of her, a perfect match.

Like she'd been born for him.

Maybe she had.

"I don't think it matters that she's a sheepherder's daughter, do you?" Allethaire cocked her head and regarded him.

He sighed against a surge of longing so intense his bones hurt. "Not a damned bit."

"Goodbye, Trey." She rose up on tiptoe and kissed his cheek. "Forget the prejudices. Don't be afraid to be happy with her."

She turned from him, then, and stepped away. Closed him out of her life. Left him behind with the clear message she didn't need him anymore.

Not that she ever did.

Don't be afraid to be happy with her.

Allethaire's perception scared the hell out of him. He was a cattleman, born and bred. What right did he have to want Zurina to overlook that and find a place for him in her life?

None. No right at all.

But he had to try. If he didn't, and soon, he could lose her forever.

He headed toward the fire, but Nubby came toward him before he got there.

"Hell of a day," the old cowboy said.

Behind him, Zurina hovered over Mikolas, like a hen over her chick. Trey hadn't known much mothering growing up, and this nurturing side of Zurina, her strong sense of family, touched him deeply.

He grunted his fervent agreement to Nubby's comment. "Sure was."

"Sutton loved your mama, Trey. Just so you know."

The words rolled through him. Left him pensive. A little sad. "I can hardly recall a time when he spoke of her."

Nubby shrugged. "Wasn't his way, I guess. But it just about killed him when she died. I figure he grieved over her the rest of his life."

Trey frowned. "He should have remarried. Found another woman to love. Would've saved a heap of trouble and hurt."

"Was never a woman for him after her." Nubby shook his grizzled head and sighed. "A man has needs, you know, and he just found other females to take care of them."

"But Zurina's *mother*, Nub." Trey would never condone the sin his father committed against her.

Nubby grimaced, lifted his hat and scratched his head.

"He was hurting. That's all I can make of it. It wasn't right, not by a long shot. We'll never know exactly what happened between them, but I suspect he was angry, too, and well, he did what he did."

Zurina and Mikolas would never forgive him, either. And they wouldn't forget.

"Did you know about Mikolas?" Trey asked quietly.

"No, I didn't. Your pa didn't, either. He would've told me." Nub hesitated. "Now, Woodrow was a different story. A real pain in the ass."

Trey recalled receiving the ransom note and Nubby's reaction to reading it. He glowered at the cowboy.

"I'm not proud I had to keep him secret from you," Nubby hastened to say. "He was your half brother, and you were entitled, but Sutton would've strung me up by my nuts if I told you. He despised that boy from the minute he first laid eyes on him, and that was when the blackmail began. Hard for Sutton to accept he'd sired such a lowlife."

Trey recalled his father's fierce pride and understood. "You still should have told me."

"It was how Sutton wanted it." No regrets. No excuses.

Hard for Trey not to feel he'd grown up like a

bird with his head in the sand. Oblivious. And protected.

But it was done, and Trey couldn't change the past, which, he reminded himself, had given him two brothers. One had been taken away, but he had Mikolas, and with him came Zurina….

Again, his gaze slid toward her. She'd already been watching him, and his pulse leaped from the knowledge. From a sudden burst of hunger.

How could he walk away from her?

She pulled her lashes down and angled her face away, but not before he glimpsed a shimmer of pain. The inevitability of what was to come.

"What do you figure will happen to Mikolas, Nub?" Trey asked roughly.

The police chief approached, holding the reins to Mikolas's horse.

"He was an accomplice to kidnapping, Trey," the lawman said grimly, answering before Nubby could. "Extortion, too. He'll have to go trial and put in jail time for it."

"Damned shame," Trey said and meant it.

"Just so you know," Nubby added, watching him. "We paid a visit to Gabirel Vasco. He told us you were headed up here to Rogers Pass."

"And none too soon," Trey said, thinking of Woodrow and how close the man had come to pulling the trigger. If the lawmen hadn't arrived when they did, lives would've been taken, long before their time.

"He loves Mikolas as his own son, but he thinks the world of you. He's hoping you'll do right by Mikolas."

Trey heard what the cowboy didn't say. That it was Trey's place to do so.

Trey wondered if he could.

Be a brother to Mikolas.

"Time to head out," George said crisply. "We'll be riding in the dark as it is."

"You'll need help getting Mikolas in the saddle," Nubby said.

"Appreciate it."

They approached the campfire, and Trey followed.

"This is going to hurt that leg like the dickens, Mikolas, but we'll be as careful as we can," George said. "Are you ready?"

"Yes."

"Goodbye, Mikolas." Zurina flung her arms around him. "Papa and I will come to see you as soon as we can. I promise."

He hugged her fiercely, then kissed her forehead. "Don't worry about me, 'Rina."

She bit her lip and blinked fast. "How can I not?"

"There's no shame in a man paying for his mistakes. It's a good thing when he learns from them at the same time." He touched her cheek, his dark eyes somber and full of regret.

"Yes," she whispered. "A good thing."

The police chief stepped toward Mikolas's right. "I'll take this side. Nubby, you take his left. We'll lift him at the same time."

But compelled by some inner force that convinced Trey it was up to him to finally begin to atone for his father's sin, that there was no one else, he nudged Nubby aside.

"I'll do it," he said.

The cowboy was quick to comply. Mikolas's startled gaze rammed into Trey's, and pride flashed up from the innermost depths. Maybe a flare of resentment, too. But as if Mikolas realized their uselessness, he roped his resistance back and nodded in concession.

"Thanks," he said.

Trey gave him a curt nod, bent and laid Mikolas's arm over his shoulder. He wasn't prepared for the effect Mikolas's quick inhalation of breath had on him. Or that his fingers dug into Trey during the ordeal. By the time they maneuvered him into the saddle with a leg flaming with fire, Trey was feeling a pretty good dose of sympathy for what the man had endured.

His brother, he corrected. What his *brother* had endured.

Trey gave George instructions to pay Doc Shehan a call as soon as they got into Great Falls. The lawman agreed.

It was much easier to get Reggie onto his horse, of course. The police chief made sure his bound wrists were tied good and tight to the saddle horn to prevent escape.

"We spotted the rustled cattle a little ways down the pass," Nubby said, pulling on his gloves. "I'll run 'em back to the ranch."

Trey knew he should offer to help. This time, he didn't.

"Thanks," he said instead.

"I'll see you, then. Tomorrow, likely."

"Tomorrow."

The old cowboy strode off to join the others, already mounted and waiting.

Only Zurina remained.

Trey turned to her. Dusk had begun to settle over the mountain. A muted spray of orange and pink curved the horizon. The pines lost their vibrant shade of green to deeper hues of shadow.

She looked incredibly beautiful standing there, in the fading light. But then, she looked beautiful in firelight, too. Or brilliant sunlight.

In any light, or none at all. She would always be beautiful to him.

"Trey, I—"

He hated this unease between them. This damned fragility. As if the air would break if either of them spoke the wrong word.

"What, Zurina?" He kept his voice low. Gentle.

She clasped her hands, then unclasped them. He couldn't recall seeing her nervous before.

"Thank you for being kind to him," she said.

He lifted a shoulder in a careless shrug. "He's my brother." His mouth curved. "Right?"

She drew in a breath, let it out again. "Yes."

"We have plenty of catching up to do," he said. "I think I'm looking forward to it."

Hope flared in her expression. "Are you?"

"He's all the family I have left, Zurina." He wanted her to understand he intended to keep his promise, that he meant every word.

Her mouth softened. "He's a sheepherder, you know."

"Yeah, well." Trey heaved an exaggerated sigh. "He'll come around eventually."

She laughed, and Trey tucked the sound away, deep into his heart.

Her amusement faded. "I almost forgot to give you this."

She reached under her sweater and pulled out a flower. The thing was so damned bent and broken with its petals half gone, he almost didn't recognize it.

The rose he'd picked from her mother's bush.

"It fell from your shirt pocket last night." She smoothed the stem carefully, as if she could make it straight and strong again. "You wanted it for Allethaire."

"No." He shook his head. "It was never for her."

She appeared taken aback. "Oh?"

"For you, Zurina," he said huskily. "I wanted the rose to remind me of you."

She pressed a hand to her breast, and her eyes welled. "Me?"

God, he ached to take her into his arms and kiss some sense into her. She meant the world to him. How could she be this surprised to know she did?

"Allethaire is leaving." Zurina darted an uncertain glance to the riders heading down the pass. Leaving the two of them behind. Her expression revealed he needed to hurry to catch up.

"I know," he said patiently. "I already told her goodbye."

"But—"

"She's going back to Minnesota. And I'm not. Never was, besides."

"But—"

"Forget Allethaire," Trey said. Firmly.

"Oh, Trey."

The turning of her head kept him from seeing her expression, but he sensed the emotion she held in tight inside her.

The hope.

The fear.

He took a step toward her.

"I love you, Zurina."

The words came far easier than he expected and of

their own accord. He hadn't realized the depth of his feelings for her until now, when it was time to leave her.

Unless she didn't want him to go.

A rawness scraped at his insides, a sudden desperation to crush the questions screaming inside them. Face them head-on and silence them forever.

To make her his for the rest of their lives.

But what if she didn't want him?

Her dark eyes appeared round and luminous in the firelight. She didn't move. She barely breathed.

Seemed his confession had robbed her of words. So he kept talking.

"I'm a cattleman, I know. You've made your feelings plain about how you feel about us, but if I work hard at it, maybe I can convince you—"

"You don't have to convince me of anything, Trey. Not anymore."

Thrown off track, he hooked his thumb in his waistband. "I don't?"

"I love you, too, you know. Even when I hated you, I loved you."

She moved closer, so close he could feel her warmth. Smell the mountain in her hair. Crave the softness of her lips.

His blood stirred, hot and deep.

"I'm only a sheepherder's daughter," she said hesitantly, as if giving him a chance to change his mind.

"And you'd make a fine wife for a cattleman," he growled. "The perfect mother for his children. I'd be proud to have you at my side, Zurina. *Proud.*"

Finally his arms opened, and he took her hard against him. She filled the well of his longings with her kisses and her love, thrilling him with the knowledge he'd have a lifetime of nights to hold her like this.

Eventually she drew back and contemplated the rose she still held in her fingers, as if she'd forgotten it was there. Trey took the flower and tossed it into the fire.

"You can take a cutting from your mother's bush and plant it alongside my house," he said. "Wherever you want. As many as you want."

"Oh, a house," she breathed in delight.

He grinned and chucked her under the chin. "Did you think I lived in a cave?"

"I've always wanted a real house, Trey."

"You'll have mine now, my sweet. We're going to make it ours forever."

She snuggled against him with a sigh of happiness. He'd give her whatever she wanted to keep her happy. Gabirel, too, and yes, Mikolas…

A pretty heavy wave of his own happiness rolled through him, leaving him giddy as a loon, and he took her mouth again. Through the fervor of their kisses, she nurtured his dreams and promised a future filled with dark-eyed children, herds of cattle and flocks of sheep.

All of it, sharing his life and his beloved Montana range.

Epilogue

A Year Later

"**D**on't turn around until I tell you, Zurina."

Hearing Trey's voice, without thinking, she began to do just that, but his quick *"Whoa, not yet, sweet, not yet,"* kept her rooted—facing the window and the new lace curtain she'd just hung.

"What? Another surprise?" she asked with a smile of growing delight.

Oh, but there had been so many surprises of late. With the little one coming in only a few weeks' time, it seemed all of Montana Territory was as excited as she and Trey were. Well-wishes and kindnesses abounded, and more gifts than any baby could ever need had streamed onto the ranch from people Zurina barely knew or had never met.

"What makes you think I have a surprise for you?" he asked, sounding wide-eyed-and-innocent.

A mysterious thud belied his words, however, and her heart swelled. He was teasing, of course. Why else would he not want her to see what he was bringing into their baby's nursery?

"I think it because you've turned me into a very pampered wife," she said.

"You're mine, and you deserve pampering."

Something scraped across the wooden floor. Her curiosity raged. Only sheer willpower kept her from spinning around to see what he was up to.

"I can't have the mother of my child lacking, can I?" he added with a low grunt of exertion.

"You've brought the rocking chair, haven't you?"

Her hands clasped in excitement. She'd been waiting for *weeks* for the precious chair to arrive in Helena, then be hauled by wagon to Great Falls and finally to the WCC.

"Maybe. Maybe not."

"The bassinette then?"

The two pieces were all that were left of the nursery suite she'd ordered from Denver. The mahogany bureau had been first to arrive, and its drawers already held stacks of neatly folded blankets, bonnets and sleeping gowns. Now that the paper-hangers had left, leaving the room enchanting with its new pastel floral walls, she'd been quick to add the finishing touch—the airy curtains she'd made herself.

All that remained was the missing furniture to make the nursery complete.

Zurina was afraid to hope.

Trey blew out a breath. "All right. You can turn around now, Zurina."

He didn't have to tell her twice, and oh, there—at last!—was her beautiful rocking chair, looking rich and frightfully expensive in polished mahogany, a striking match to the bureau with its ornately carved back and graceful arms. Emotion welled, filling her chest with a sweet ache of longing for her baby to be born so that she could hold him for hours on end in this chair, just rocking and rocking...

A cradle stood next to it, and her joy faded into confusion.

"This isn't what we bought, Trey. It's a wooden cradle," she said.

"I know."

"But we bought a white iron *bassinette*."

"I was hoping you'd prefer this instead."

He didn't meet her glance, and she puzzled over his discomfiture. Was he feeling guilty for changing the style of bed they'd first chosen for their baby? It wasn't like him not to consult her first, and on this, a matter that meant so much to her. She couldn't recall seeing the cradle before in any catalog she'd scoured, either, which was just as perplexing, and why had he been so secretive all this time?

"Where did it come from?" She moved closer. Her glance fastened over the spindles, dark and gleaming in the window light. The unmistakable scent of varnish wafted through the nursery.

"It was mine."

Taken aback, she studied the baby bed in new fascination. She tried to imagine her tall, handsome, broad-shouldered husband small enough to once fit on the miniature mattress.

There came that emotion again, tumbling through her chest.

Reaching out, she gave the bed a gentle, testing nudge. It quietly swayed, back and forth, back and forth. Entranced, she fell in love.

"It's been in the attic for years," Trey said. "I moved it to the barn a while back and stripped it down to bare wood." He shifted, one foot to the other. "Your rocker came, same time as the bureau did, but I kept it from you so I could match up the stain. I thought you'd like it better that way." He hesitated, as if he hoped he'd done the right thing. "Matched up with the rest of the suite."

"Oh, Trey," she breathed, deeply moved, and recalled all those evenings he was gone of late. Now the plethora of excuses he'd given her made sense. "Your little bed is absolutely perfect for our baby."

The cradle stopped rocking. She turned toward him. "But why didn't you tell me sooner?"

"Because my father built it, Zurina. And I know how you feel about him."

She went still. She didn't think about Sutton Wells so much anymore. Woodrow Baldwin's confession to his murder quieted the rumors and ended speculation throughout the territory. Learning the truth had ended an ugly chapter in all their lives.

More important, with her marriage to Trey came acceptance. The past couldn't be changed, and Trey couldn't be blamed for any of it. She wasn't going to let what his father had done to Mama cast a shadow on her happiness. Her future.

But knowing Sutton had built this sweet little cradle for his baby all those years ago formed a different image of the man in Zurina's mind. A loving father, anticipating the birth of his child. Working long hours fashioning the wood with his hands, his heart and soul. In that bed rested his dreams for a family. His legacy.

Now, his grandchild would carry them on.

"He enjoyed carpentry," Trey said, his voice somber. "He loved building things."

Zurina cocked her head, much preferring to remember Sutton in this new way. "Like the Wells Cattle Company."

"He made mistakes along the way." Trey frowned.

She knew he thought of her mother. Mikolas, too. "Yes."

"Guess they all happened for a reason."

The troubled shadows in his copper-flecked eyes struck a sympathetic chord in Zurina. Was it the cradle which brought out his melancholy mood? Did the impending birth of their child remind him of all his father would miss?

"The mistakes brought us together as man and wife. Without them, we wouldn't have each other," she said quietly.

She moved toward him, and his arms opened easily to take her against him. She rested her cheek against his shoulder and curled her arms around his strong back. Her lashes drifted closed, and she soaked in the warmth of his body. His male scent, so familiar. So pleasing.

"Our baby will know the many good things his grandpapa has done, Trey," she said firmly. "Our forgiveness will make speaking of the bad things unnecessary."

Zurina could feel the tension seep from his muscles. His embrace tightened.

"I love you, Zurina. I wish he was here so he could see how complete you've made me."

She lifted her head, peeped at him beneath her lashes and turned coy. "If only my mother could be here, too. She'd be amazed how a cattleman could make a sheepherder's daughter so happy."

He chuckled. His head lowered, and his mouth found hers in a lazy kiss of agreement. Of sublime satisfaction. He took his time in showing her how much happiness he would give her for the rest of their lives.

As if their little one could feel their joy and wanted to remind them he was a factor in it, he wiggled and stretched in Zurina's womb. Without breaking their kiss, Trey laid a gentle hand over her swollen belly in acknowledgment.

"Excuse me, Mrs. Wells."

Zurina ended the kiss and drew back at her housekeeper's reluctant interruption. Even now, it felt strange to be called that. *Mrs. Wells.* A name which inspired so much respect. And, oh, how she loved being addressed by her husband's name.

Trey straightened, and his hand fell away. Both turned toward the woman hovering in the doorway.

As wife of one of the WCC cowboys, Rita Clementson held her position in the Wells household in high esteem. Middle-aged, slender and with strands of gray just beginning to show along her hairline, she was one of the hardest working women Zurina had ever known.

Trey had insisted Zurina have help during the last weeks before their baby's arrival. At first, Zurina dismissed the notion for its silly extravagance, citing she loved her house so much, she gladly did every chore required in its upkeep. But her stubborn husband prevailed, and in the time since, Zurina had grown to appreciate Rita's efficiency.

"I'm sorry to intrude," Rita said. "But they're coming. I figured you'd want to know."

Mikolas! Zurina's pulse leaped in anticipation. "Oh, yes. Of course I do."

Her brother's sentence in the territorial prison was over. He'd paid the price for his part in Allethaire's kidnapping, and for long, worrisome months, Zurina had prayed he would come to accept being Sutton Wells's bastard son.

Initially it seemed he never would, but eventually, he began to respond to her weekly letters. And with every one, he sounded more and more like the brother she remembered.

Still, it wouldn't be easy for him to come here. To the WCC. But Zurina had insisted, and so had Trey. Papa, too, and well, with no other choice, Mikolas had reluctantly agreed.

For days, Zurina had been getting ready for him. With Rita's help, she'd prepared the extra bedroom, cleaned the house until the floors and furniture shined and cooked the Basque foods that had always been his favorites. She looked forward to seeing him eat his fill, but how would he act when he arrived? Would he be resentful? Unhappy?

After the housekeeper left, Trey twined his fingers with hers. "Don't be nervous."

"I can't help it."

"We'll need time to get used to one another again, that's all."

"I hope it doesn't take too long. For Mikolas, I mean."

Giving her fingers a reassuring squeeze, Trey led her from the nursery. She cast a lingering glance over the beautiful new cradle and rocking chair. There'd be time enough later to arrange them just right.

"He wouldn't be here if he didn't want to be, at least, deep down," Trey said.

Despite the practicality of his words, however, Zurina fussed at the impression Mikolas would have of her new life with Trey. Her new home. A cattleman's house, two levels tall and with more bedrooms than any Basque family would have.

Would he find it too pretentious? Would he resent her for leaving the poor simplicity of Papa's tiny cabin in the hills for the house of her dreams?

She descended the stairs, her free hand trailing along the smooth, polished handrail. On the way down, her gaze absorbed the thick, floral carpets adorning each room. The dark, solid furniture, too. As solid and strong as Trey Wells himself.

She loved every inch, every piece, every moment in her house. If Mikolas didn't approve, well, there was nothing more she could do to change his mind. She'd worked through her prejudices and found more happiness with Trey than she ever thought possible.

She only hoped Mikolas would work through his prejudices, too.

Through the glass, she glimpsed three riders approaching. In light of her delicate condition, Dr. Shehan forbade her from journeying to meet her brother's train. Papa and Uncle Benat had gone without her, leaving Deunoro to watch over her father's new flock, grazing in Sun River Valley. If not for the generosity of her husband, Papa would never have been able to start over again, but Trey's loan allowed him to continue to afford caring for the sheep he loved so much.

"Are you ready?" Trey halted at the door, his hand on the knob.

As long as she had Trey, she'd be ready for anything. She would always be content, living with him, right where she needed to be, and on impulse, she rose up on tiptoe and kissed his lips.

"Of course," she said.

He slid his arm around her waist, and together, they went outside to wait on the porch for the three men in her family to draw near. They pulled up in the yard, and her gaze fastened over her brother. He appeared thinner, paler. His hair was shorter, his clothes new and unfamiliar. But he was home, and he was free, and before she knew it, she found herself in his arms, held carefully in his embrace.

"It is good to see you again, 'Rina," he murmured in a fervent voice. He stepped back, as if he feared he'd hurt her baby if he held her too long or too close.

Zurina stood perfectly still and endured his inspecting gaze. Her heart pounded from worry that he would find contempt in what he saw. A powerful cattleman's wife. His half brother's wife, too.

Mikolas would notice she wore her hair differently now, swept up in the latest style, according to the drawings in her favorite magazine, *Harper's Bazaar*. When his perusal lowered, he would see how she'd developed a passion for fashion as well. Her russet sateen wrapper with its pleated folds and fitted bodice trimmed in black velvet was as fine as could be found in the territory. Yet when his gaze touched on her rounded belly, his attention jumped over to Trey.

Who stood waiting for his reaction with his feet braced and his gaze direct. As if he challenged Mikolas to defame the new life he'd made with Zurina as her husband.

"Hello, Mikolas," Trey said.

Her brother acknowledged the greeting with a slow nod. "Trey."

"Welcome home."

Mikolas swallowed. His scrutiny dragged off Trey and slid over the expansive ranch before him. The yard with its clipped lawn already a deep spring-green. The barn. The bunkhouse. Sheds and corrals. Farther out, more cattle on the range than a man could quickly count. Horses, too. The snow-topped

Bear Tooth Mountains sprawled beyond them, under a crisp azure sky that never ended.

Looking overwhelmed, he pulled his gaze back again. Pride shone in his jet-black eyes.

"It's not mine to call—" he began.

"In time, Mikolas." Trey's voice rumbled with understanding. With certainty. "Just give it some time."

Zurina held her breath, sensing the demons her brother fought. Again his glance lifted, this time to the large square window on the far left side of the house.

He would be forever haunted by the night Sutton was murdered in his office, she knew. Though Mikolas was innocent of the killing, he would never forget. He would always wish that his actions, his intentions, had been different.

Perhaps, in time, he would forgive himself for what Woodrow had done. Time that would help him bury the ugliness of the past and encourage him to look forward to the future.

To accept the Wells legacy as his own.

And when better to begin his new future than now?

Zurina slid her arm under Trey's, then extended her hand toward Mikolas.

"Come," she said softly. "We have much to talk about."

For a long moment, he didn't move.

"It's your place, Mikolas," Trey urged. "To be here with us."

As if their words conquered his trepidation, he took Zurina's hand in a tight clasp.

"Yes," he said.

She drew him closer to her side. Together, the three of them turned and headed toward the house. But before climbing the stairs, she paused and tossed a questioning glance back toward the pair waiting on horseback.

"Papa? Uncle Benat? Aren't you coming?" she asked.

Trey grinned. "You'd best hurry. She's fixing sausages for supper."

Her father's eyes lit up. *"Txistorras?"*

"Our mouths water at the thought of them, eh, Gabirel?" Uncle Benat said, swinging his girth out of the saddle. "The sheep can wait."

Zurina laughed, climbed the steps and strolled into her house. The men followed right behind.

She would always be a sheepherder's daughter, but she reveled most in being a cattleman's wife. Their lives had merged. They'd become one.

They'd become a family.

* * * * *

HISTORICAL

HISTORICAL

HER DARK AND DANGEROUS LORD
by Anne Herries

Exiled Lord Stefan de Montfort rescues Englishwoman
Anne Melford from the sea and takes her to his château
in Normandy. Anne fires within Stefan a disturbing,
forbidden desire. Could such a lady ever marry a dark
and dangerous scoundrel like him?

SIERRA BRIDE
by Jenna Kernan

Wealthy Sam Pickett is used to getting his way. So he is
baffled when Kate Wells, a feisty little hellion who steps
between him and a bullet, isn't interested in becoming
his wife. If he can't make her his bride, then he'll
most certainly make her his mistress!

BREATHLESS
by Anne Stuart

Ruined beyond repair and shunned by London society,
Miranda Rohan rebelliously embraces the freedom of having
nothing left to lose. This dangerous course throws her under
the power of the darkly enigmatic Lucien de Malheur—
known as the Scorpion...
The House of Rohan

On sale from 4th March 2011
Don't miss out!

*Available at WHSmith, Tesco, ASDA, Eason
and all good bookshops*
www.millsandboon.co.uk

04a

0211/04b

REGENCY

Collection

*Let these sparklingly seductive delights whirl
you away to the ballrooms—and
bedrooms—of Polite Society!*

Volume 1 – 4th February 2011
Regency Pleasures by Louise Allen

Volume 2 – 4th March 2011
Regency Secrets by Julia Justiss

Volume 3 – 1st April 2011
Regency Rumours by Juliet Landon

Volume 4 – 6th May 2011
Regency Redemption by Christine Merrill

Volume 5 – 3rd June 2011
Regency Protectors by Margaret McPhee

Volume 6 – 1st July 2011
Regency Improprieties by Diane Gaston

12 volumes in all to collect!

MILLS & BOON

www.millsandboon.co.uk

2 FREE BOOKS
AND A SURPRISE GIFT

We would like to take this opportunity to thank you for reading this Mills & Boon® book by offering you the chance to take TWO more specially selected books from the Historical series absolutely FREE! We're also making this offer to introduce you to the benefits of the Mills & Boon® Book Club™—

- **FREE home delivery**
- **FREE gifts and competitions**
- **FREE monthly Newsletter**
- **Exclusive Mills & Boon Book Club offers**
- **Books available before they're in the shops**

Accepting these FREE books and gift places you under no obligation to buy, you may cancel at any time, even after receiving your free books. Simply complete your details below and return the entire page to the address below. You don't even need a stamp!

YES Please send me 2 free Historical books and a surprise gift. I understand that unless you hear from me, I will receive 4 superb new books every month for just £3.99 each, postage and packing free. I am under no obligation to purchase any books and may cancel my subscription at any time. The free books and gift will be mine to keep in any case.

Ms/Mrs/Miss/Mr ———————— Initials ————————

Surname ————————————————————

Address ————————————————————

———————————————— Postcode ————————

E-mail ————————————————————

Send this whole page to: Mills & Boon Book Club, Free Book Offer, FREEPOST NAT 10298, Richmond, TW9 1BR

Offer valid in UK only and is not available to current Mills & Boon Book Club subscribers to this series. Overseas and Eire please write for details.. We reserve the right to refuse an application and applicants must be aged 18 years or over. Only one application per household. Terms and prices subject to change without notice. Offer expires 30th April 2011. As a result of this application, you may receive offers from Harlequin Mills & Boon and other carefully selected companies. If you would prefer not to share in this opportunity please write to The Data Manager, PO Box 676, Richmond, TW9 1WU.

Mills & Boon® is a registered trademark owned by Harlequin Mills & Boon Limited. The Mills & Boon® Book Club™ is being used as a trademark.